THE BATTLE BETWEEN LIGHT AND DARK

Kelsie took heart as she saw one shadow fade, another break suddenly into bits as if it were tangible and could be handled.

Then—

Out from the columns came a beam of fierce red to strike full upon the whirling crystals of the jewels. Their clear light clouded—what was white and gold became red and darkened. The shadows on the surface of the world took heart, gathered, spread, ate up more and more of the land.

Kelsie cried out . . .

THE GATE OF THE CAT
Andre Norton

"THE GATE OF THE CAT will please fans of this series; it measures up well to the standards set in her recent novels."

—*Science Fiction Chronicle*

ANDRE NORTON

THE GATE OF THE CAT

ACE BOOKS, NEW YORK

With gratitude for Ingrid without whose help this book would never have come to be.

THE GATE OF THE CAT

An Ace Book / published by arrangement with
the author

PRINTING HISTORY
Ace hardcover edition / October 1987
Ace edition / July 1988

ISBN: 0-441-27380-7

Ace Books are published by The Berkley Publishing Group,
200 Madison Avenue, New York, New York 10016.
The name "ACE" and the "A" logo are trademarks belonging to
Charter Communications, Inc.

10 9 8 7 6 5 4 3 2 1

One

The long evening twilight pulled pools of shadows from small bushes. Kelsie shivered though she was warm enough in the quilted coat and the thick slacks above boots which seemed to sink a little more at every step she took over the reach of peaty soil which lay between her and the rise of the mist-crowned hills beyond. It was to her an unreal, even threatening landscape, yet she was far from turning back. She set her teeth and tightened her grip on the small basket she carried. Maybe tonight she would succeed; she refused to give up and accept all their stories.

At the present she saw nothing beautiful or imposing in the land about her, for all the gushing of the travel brochures on which she had first built her ideas of what was to be found and seen in these far northern Scottish highlands. Instead, she had the feeling of tramping over a deserted land in which some invisible menace lay in wait. One could well believe in Black Dogs and Daft Ponies out of Hell, of the meddling of otherworld things hereabout. Goodness knew there were stories enough—and she had listened to them eagerly when they had been told about the fireside. Only this was not the safety of a room lit and undercover.

She listened apprehensively to the noises of the night.

There was the bark of a vixen, a distant answering howl from some farm dog. In answer to that stark loneliness, which those cries only accentuated, she hummed under her breath. It was the wordless up and down of notes that she always used when she confronted injured or frightened animals. Injured— She felt again the white hot stab of rage which had filled her two days ago when she had seen that torturous trap and, caught in it, ragged, blood-stained toe pads—two pads of a cat's paw gnawed purposefully to give the captured freedom.

Good for nothing they said—to be hunted down before the next lambing season if possible. That Neil McAdams had been very sure of himself about that!

Only she had seen the predator. It was a female, close to kittening. This past day under better light she had traced it up into the wilderness of the hillside. The grouse were thick and she had started up a whole covey, which was doubtless against the strange laws of this place also—

Kelsie set her lips obstinately together as she remembered the parts of fireside talk which she had not relished. The hunting down of a five point stag— Culling (as they called it—why not say what it really was—murder of the innocent) of the deer herd last year. The hunting drives to send birds into the air to be shot for sport—sport!

At least she knew in time she would never fit in here. She would put the house up for sale and—

Up ahead a tall shadow dislodged itself from a clump of brush and moved purposefully in the same direction she was going. There was no mistaking either the nature of the elongated part of that shadow—a man with a gun. And what he hunted here would be—

Kelsie began to run forward. This was still her land and certainly she would have the privilege to say who would come on it, and a right to distrust the motives of any skulker.

She saw ahead the standing stones—they called them that though all but three had been overthrown by the church in the old days. As a lesson to those who clung to the old times and ways, a warning later for those who might meddle in the forbidden. The three which still stood forming a rough arch, one mighty stone of crudely hewn rock balanced on two of its fellows. It was toward that that the intruder was walking.

She was nearly abreast of him now.

Of course it was Neil. Somehow she had known that from the first. The trap had failed so now he would hunt down a wounded animal and use that gun— On her land, never!

There was a wailing sound from beyond. Pain in it as well as feral hatred and determination to be free. The man raised his gun and Kelsie threw herself forward, but tripped. It was only her upflung arm which jarred against his so that when he shot the charge went wild.

"What do you do!" There was hot anger in his voice but Kelsie's attention was beyond—the squat shape drawn in upon itself, huddled in the very center of that archway. The wildcat—perhaps too injured to run, facing them both with hatred and the determination to fight to the death.

"Stop it!" Kelsie was breathless as she regained her feet. "Leave the poor thing alone! Haven't you tormented it enough by now?"

"Stop it, girl!" he snarled angrily back. "Yon beast is vermin. It will savage lambs in the spring—"

He was raising the rifle again just as the moon broke through one of the twilight clouds full upon the arch and the cat crouched in it. This time Kelsie was more surely footed. She dropped her basket and snatched for the gun with both hands. He fended her off and her foot turned on some stone deep buried in the turf. As his fist cracked against the side of her face she spun out and around, voicing a cry of protest and anger, and then fell into the arch from which the injured cat sprang but a second before. As her head hit against the stone Kelsie rolled forward through the same opening into the place of the fallen rocks.

* * *

Kelsie was first aware of the warmth. Without opening her eyes she twisted a little so that her face felt the full heat. That small movement sent pain shooting through her head and she cried out. There was movement beside her shoulder, a rough surface rasped across her cheek. At last she opened her eyes and then blinked rapidly as a full force of sun beamed down upon her.

She had a confused memory of falling and then darkness. But surely this was not night in the Scottish foothills—this was day! Had she been hurt and just lain there? And Neil! She propped herself up on one elbow and looked around.

This—how had she come here? Those stones, which had been age buried when she had fallen in among them, were now set up guardian straight. A warmth radiated from the nearest against which she had lain. The stand of grass within that circle was not the stubby, coarse growth she had known, but was even closer to the earth and patched with what seemed to be moss. What did spring higher was spangled with flowers of a cream white, cupped like tulips, except they were not like any tulips she had ever seen. Among them fluttered insects with bright wings.

"Rrrrrowww—" Again she turned her head, so suddenly that pain brought another cry from her. The wildcat crouched there, licking its torn foot, but looking now and again to her as if it perfectly understood that she could help it.

Her basket lay a foot or so away and she stretched out an arm to grasp it, each movement bringing that sickening pain in her head. With one hand she gingerly explored her own skin and hair on that side. There was the ooze of liquid and she brought away fingers painted the bright red of blood. She could only explore by the lightest of touches but she believed that the cut was a small one, more of a rasping and bruising of skin than the larger wound she had expected.

Fumbling with the contents of her basket she brought out

the antibiotic salve and the cotton swabs she had carried on her mission of mercy. These she shared equally with the cat who only growled warningly as she handled its foot and smeared on the same protective jelly as she had used on her own left temple.

It was still difficult to move. Any sudden change in the position of her head not only brought a stab of pain but a feeling of nausea. So, when she had done with her battlefield surgery for them both, she leaned her back against one of those standing stones, which had so unbelievably raised itself from the ground, to look about her with more intent interest. The cat crouched some distance away again, licking its torn paw but showing no desire to withdraw further.

Now that she had time to observe—to think of more than her immediate plight, she studied what lay before her with eyes narrowed against the glare of the sun. She had already shed her coat because of the unnatural heat and now wished she could slip out of her heavy turtleneck sweater into the bargain.

Surely this was not even the brightest of summer days such as she had heretofore known on Ben Blair. Nor were the flowers, rippling gently under the teasing fingers of a light breeze, any she had seen before. And the stones—how had they come to be set upright?

Of course this might be all illusion and she still lay back in the night twilight with her battered head against the stone which had so roughly met her fall. Yet—it seemed so real!

The wildcat stopped her licking and made a small sound deep in her throat. She limped over to the coat Kelsie had abandoned and pawed at it intently as if searching the padded surface for something of her own.

Kelsie did not try to fight the vast fatigue which had settled on her when she had finished the last of her nurse-care. She closed her eyes and then opened them suddenly twice, as if she tried to catch the landscape before her in the midst of some change. However, it remained always the same—the standing bluish stones, the patches of flowers, the unnatural heat. She began to feel thirsty.

Now if she were indeed on the slope of Ben Blair there should be a spring not many paces away from the place of stones. The very thought of water curling out of the ground made her run her tongue over lips suddenly even more dry. Water—

She did not try to stand up, even creeping on her hands and knees made her feel qualms of nausea. However, she forced herself across a quarter of the circle, out between the stones, in the general direction where that spring must lie.

Only there was no spring, at least none where she sought. She slipped down again to lie full length in the midst of a patch of the wild flowers, the perfume of which was so strong as to add to her illness.

Water—with every moment she craved a drink more. Now it seemed she could actually hear it. Perhaps she had not been headed in the right direction. Muzzily she somehow once more got to her hands and knees heading south. Moments later she was indeed looking at water— down into water, for here was a steep falling away of the land above a pool which mothered a small rill trickling away among moss grown rocks.

In spite of falling painfully once, Kelsie reached the edge of that pool and cupped her hands to drink liquid as chill as if it had just been imprisoned by ice. Still the chill cleared her head a little and she slapped more of it on her face, avoiding the edge of the cut. Until, for the first time since she had awakened, she felt wholly herself again.

There was no such pool on Ben Blair, just as the standing stones had been lying once there. Where was she? Still wandering in the depths of some hallucination produced by the blow on her head? She must not panic, and panic came from just such thoughts and questions without answers. For the moment she seemed to be herself even if the rest of the world had changed.

She pulled out the shirt she had worn under her sweater

and soaked it in the cold water, wringing it as dry as she could before tying it around her head. For the first time she became aware of a twittering and flitting at the other side of the pool. There was a bush there bending under a burden of dark red berries and birds were feasting, showing no interest in her at all.

Not grouse, nor any others she had seen before. There was one species with a golden breast and wings of a muted rose color, another a vivid green-blue, such plumage as she had seen before only on the throats of peacocks.

Berries—food—

Just as the need for water had risen in her so now came the need to appease a hunger. She edged around the water. The birds fluttered a little away but did not rise on the wing as she had expected them to do. She drew a hand down one dangling branch and harvested a full palm's load of the berries. They were sweet, yet had a lingering tartness which somehow added to their flavor, and, having tasted, she straightway set about gathering and cramming into her mouth all she could reach and snatch from the same branches where some birds were still boldly feeding.

Two or three of those with the metallic blue feathers had withdrawn a little and were watching her—not as if they feared any move or attack on her part, but rather as if she herself provided some kind of puzzle they must solve. At length one of them took off, soaring up into the sky, the sun making a rich glory of its wings.

The cat— Kelsie looked at the birds, some of whom were eating fearlessly only a hand's distance from her. She wondered if the creature was worse injured than she had thought, and she turned to make her way back to that inexplainable circle of stone pillars. The upward slope she took cautiously, now back on her feet to feel the ground swaying under her. Then she reached the top of that rise and looked ahead. There was the yellowish-black patch of her discarded coat and she stumbled her way back to it, concentrating on the garment rather than what stood around it.

There came a tiny mewling cry as her shadow fell across the edge of the coat and an instant answering growl. Then she saw the kittens—two of them, small, blind shapes which the cat had just finished washing.

She knew better than to approach too closely, that growl had sunk to a low sound in the mother's throat but that she would allow an interference with her family Kelsie doubted. She spoke softly, using the same words that she had used many times over at Dr. Atless's when she had been the attendant in his veterinary hospital.

"Good girl, clever girl—" she squatted down, with her back to one of the stones, to survey the small family. "You have pretty kittens—good girl—"

She was startled then by a cry which certainly had not come from the cat or her new family. It might have been the howling of a tormented dog, only Kelsie's knowledge of dogs said no to that. Twice it sounded. The cat's ears flattened to her skull, her eyes became warning slits. Kelsie shivered even under the strong beams of that sun. She faced outward from the circle toward the heights which lay beyond. For the third time that cry sounded and it was certainly nearer and sharper, as if a hunter were hot upon a trail. The girl looked about her for a weapon, some hope of defense. At last she tugged at the coat on which the cat had bedded down, loosing the belt and drawing it out. With no stick nor stone here that was her only possible choice.

At the fourth howl the creature who had so given tongue came into sight—first only a black blot padding out of a stand of brush. And then, as it came closer, Kelsie had difficulty in stifling a cry. A dog?

No, no hound that she had ever heard of or seen resembled this! It was almost skeleton thin, the ridges of its ribs plainly visible beneath its shiny skin. A mouth which appeared to split two thirds of its skull dropped open and a scarlet tongue lolled out, saliva and whitish foam dripping from it. The long legs seemed only bones with skin stretched tightly over them as it padded forward, not with a rush but steadily as if it had marked its prey and had no idea of losing it now.

Kelsie pulled herself up, one shoulder against the pillar, the buckle end of her belt dangling loose, the other end wrapped tightly about her hand lest she lose her hold on it. She heard a growl and glanced for a moment at the cat. The kittens were half hidden under her body where fur bristled up in challenge. Though she visibly leaned her weight mostly on her uninjured paw, it was plain she was prepared to do battle.

The hound did not leap forward as Kelsie expected. Instead it stopped while still several feet away from the pillared circle. Throwing back its narrow head the beast gave vent once more to its chilling bay as if summoning some companion of the hunt. Though she and the cat were weak enough, Kelsie thought with fiercely beating heart, to give but token defense.

There was an answer to that last bay, a cry which was not a similar howl but rather more like a call in words she could not understand. Then out of the same knot of brush which had concealed the dog creature came a horse and rider. The girl drew a startled, shaken breath.

The horse, or whatever that beast was, showed as much a walking rack of bones as the hound. In its skull the eyes were pits of whirling greenish-yellow flame. While the rider was cloaked, so enveloped in a muffling covering that could not say what manner of thing it might really be. But it was plain that this newcomer had eyes for and interest in her. One begloved hand raised a rod and swung it in her direction with the same calm assurance which McAdams had shown toward shooting the cat.

Kelsie did not even have time to put the stone between her and that crooked dash of flame which sprang from the rod. Only it did not strike her. To her overwhelming surprise it was as if that meant-to-be flash of fire struck an impenetrable wall a little before the stone—sprayed out in a red burst and was gone, leaving a trail of oily smoke to rise in the clear sky.

The hound howled and began to run, not straight for the girl, but circling about the stones as if it sought some door or opening which would let it at its would-be victims. For a moment or two the rider was motionless. Then he used reins and swung the head of his mount to the left joining the hound in that circling of what might be a fortress the twain of them could not best.

Kelsie held tight with one hand to the stone beside her but also turned her head and then her body to watch the encirclement. She had had no trouble leaving the circle nor returning to it, but these two beyond now appeared totally walled away.

In her mind bewilderment fast became panic and fear. Where was she? She could not be anywhere but in some hospital racked with wild hallucinations because of the blow on her head. But this was so real—!

The hound gave tongue continually, almost querulously, as if it could not understand what kept it away from the two inside the circle.

However, the rider remained where he was, his mount now and then nervously pawing the earth but held firmly in check. That rod was handled negligently, its tip pointed earthward. It would seem that they were under siege, perhaps being held for the coming of some even greater menace. Yet when the next stroke arrived it was not Kelsie who was aroused to front the danger but the snarling wildcat.

Within the circle of the rock a moss covered patch of earth heaved upward and burst into separate sods as if from some explosion below. Out of the cascadng earth pushed what looked like a bird's beak, a sickly yellow-gray, and from beside Kelsie the wildcat sprang into action.

Her leap carried her farther on so that she was behind that questing beak and in spite of her injured foot she used both forepaws to land them together on a thing struggling up from the burrow it had made.

There was a whirl of furred body and a slapping length of what looked mostly like a land-going lobster. Then the cat's teeth met with a crunch just behind the end of the beak, and, though the many-legged thing went on flopping, it was clearly out of the battle. The cat settled down over it, tearing loose clawed limbs and worrying at the thing's underbelly until she passed its chitinous armor to the flesh beneath, which she ate as if famished. However, Kelsie, so warned by its appearance from the earth made the rounds of the circle, searching the ground intently for any other suspicious tumbling of the soil.

She came upon one such near across the circle from the still-feasting cat and made ready with her belt. The narrow tip of that beak or nose which quested for the upper world thrust through a clump of the flowers and she lashed her belt at it. More by luck than any skill the loop of the buckle did fall about that tip and she gave a vicious jerk, putting into that all her power of arm.

As a fish that had swallowed a hook the thing came out of the ground flopping over on its back, sharply clawed feet waving in the air. But the rising had also freed a long, jointed tail which ended in what could only be a sting. That snapped back and forth evilly while the creature's head, flipping from side to side freed it from the buckle, it arose again, seeming to turn in midair to land on its feet. For a moment only it hesitated and then it leaped, springing at least three feet from the torn flowers to aim straight at Kelsie.

She swung the belt a second time, managing again to strike and so ward off attack. But, as she also retreated, she came sharply back against one of the blue pillars and was caught up in something else, a sharp tingling of her body such as one might receive from a minor electrical shock.

Her left hand clawed at the stone which was not cold, as she had expected, but rather held a warmth which appeared to be growing. In doing so she rasped her fingers upon a protrusion of the rock which broke away into her hand.

There was one chance now. She could not even have told from whence came that saving idea but she pulled in her belt and worked the stone into the buckle, wedging it so with all her might, her attention all for the many-legged creature out of the earth and her fingers working by touch alone.

It was the cat who gave her the few precious seconds out of time to do that. Having finished with the carcass of the first of their attackers it was now creeping up behind the other. Then Kelsie struck, this time with careful aim and intent purpose.

The weighted buckle met the creature in midair for it had sprung again even as she had swung. There was a flash of brilliant light and a puff of smoke, a nauseating odor which made her retch. The thing struck the ground charred and black. It might have been tossed through a blazing fire. Kelsie was so heartened by the success of her desperate hope that she turned to claw again at the pillar behind her, striving to free more such useful bits of rock. But it would seem that luck or chance had loosened only that one for her aid.

Snarling, the cat drew back from the charred curl of body and leaped now for Kelsie's coat where it settled down, drawing close to its body, with a sweep of foreleg, the two squeaking kittens.

Neither the hound nor the rider had made any move during that odd battle and now they showed no dismay that it had not succeeded—if the earth dwellers were allies of theirs after all. It appeared that they were willing to wait— either for their prey to be somehow shaken out as a nut is shaken out of a broken shell, or for more efficient reinforcements.

Time, Kelsie thought, did not favor her or the cat. There would be another attack of sorts—or she would wake from this dream which was so real that the fear of it nearly paralyzed her if she allowed herself to consider it.

She continued to absently rub one hand along the rough surface of the stone, her attention going from hound to rider and back again—waiting for what would happen next.

There came a clear trilling call out of the air overhead. The hound was on its feet, snarling, leaping now and then. Kelsie saw winging back and forth over the animal was one of those blue birds which had watched her eat by the berry bushes.

From her left there came a harsh grating sound which to her ears bore no resemblance to speech. The rider had brought around his skeleton mount and now he lifted his rod and tried to aim at the darting birds, but the shooting flames were ever far behind their swift turns, fast swoops, and soarings.

Two

The cat's head was up, it was staring south to another roll of hills. Now the rider, so hood muffled that Kelsie had never seen his face, turned halfway in the saddle to face the same direction. The birds uttered sharp high cries and began a flight pattern which encircled the stones. With a sharp jerk the rider pulled at the reins and his mount plunged forward as if to bring it and its rider down upon Kelsie. But it did not complete that charge. Instead the mount reared and the rider seemed for a moment to be fighting—his will against his mount's. The hound crouched closer to the ground, near creeping on its belly back the way it had come. Though Kelsie watched carefully there was nothing else in sight save the wheeling birds.

The rider no longer fought his horse (if such a creature could be termed a horse). He allowed it to swing around to the direction from which they had come. Then, though he did not seem to be urging it, the creature first broke into a trot and raised that to a gallop as it disappeared in a cut between two of the hills, the hound now running beside it.

Kelsie waited. The birds broke off their circling to fly east. She and the cat were alone in the circle of pillars which had indeed proved a sanctuary.

The girl slipped to the ground, sitting cross-legged near

her coat where the kittens now nursed—the cat having relaxed enough to allow them to her.

For the first time since she had awakened, Kelsie had a chance to think clearly, to look more slowly about her, to weigh one strange thing against its neighbor. She had been struggling with Neil McAdams in the long summer twilight of the Scottish highlands. But it was plain that where she now was bore no relation to that. She raised her fingertips to smooth the damp shirt she had tied over her head wound. It was all so real—

Slowly she pulled herself once more to her feet and began to make a complete circuit of the circle, looking outward for a point of reference which would assure her that she was still in the world she knew or at least recognized a little. She was not even of highland blood—even if she bore the name and had the heritage from Great-Aunt Ellen she had never been here before. She belonged back in Evart, Indiana, ready to start for the animal clinic, to dream her own private dream of somehow raising the money to get a veterinarian's degree. That was the world of people and things she understood. This was not. She swung the stone-weighted belt and tried to arrange her thoughts in a logical pattern. One minute she had been struggling with Neil to keep him from shooting the already injured wildcat and then she had awakened here—

She wanted to run, to scream out her denial, to awaken from this nightmare. It went on and on and it was indeed so real. She could not remember ever having eaten and drunk in any dream before but the stains of the berries still were on her hands and she could taste their sweetness when she ran her tongue over her teeth. She looked to the cat who lay nursing the two kittens. The animal was believable. But the hound, the rider, and all that had happened since she had been besieged here—those were out of some fantasy.

None of the distant, mist veiled mountains looked familiar. Also who had raised the fallen pillars to make this fortress to what it must once have been, a circle of protection?

The cat arose, shook off her two clinging offspring and came to stand before Kelsie, regarding her straightly as somehow she had never seen an animal eye her before. It was as if an intelligence which was equal, or at least close, to her own looked out of those eyes and that some desire for communication moved the animal.

Kelsie knelt and held out one hand to the cat.

"Where are we, old girl?" she asked and then wished she had not, for her words sounded queerly here as if they had been picked up by one stone and echoed to the next and the next, coming back to her, not clearly, but in a hoarse whisper.

The cat extended a tongue tip and touched it to the girl's thumb. And she knew a glow of triumph. So a wildcat could not be tamed—so much for all they had told her when she had spoken up for the animal last night. Last night? She shook her head and then wished that she had not, for the pain which flashed outward. She was suddenly tired. Better to lie down here on the moss and just rest a little. If she slept so much the better, she might then awaken in her own place and time.

Only there was to be no rest. The wildcat suddenly yowled and Kelsie wondered, even as she clapped her hands over both of her ears, if the animal had sensed the same dislocation as she did now. This was a different kind of pain than that which had driven her since her awaking here. It was like a cry for help so intense and demanding that the girl was on her feet, stumbling back through that gate to answer it.

Back through the gate but not to her own place. The land about her remained the same. Her shuffle became a run as she was drawn on. She was aware of the furry shape which followed in her shadow, also pulled perhaps by that demanding cry which she knew now, but could not understand how, rang within her head not outside through her ears.

Together cat and girl rounded a heap of moss-grown stones which might have been the remains of some very ancient ruin not treated as well by time as the pillars behind. Kelsie skidded down the dale, the belt swinging in her hand ready to use. What they came upon were the signs of tragedy. Three forms lay there, a soaking of blood curling from between their shoulders where upstanding feathered shafts proclaimed arrows. Arrows!

The girl's startlement at that was gone in an instant when she saw the fourth member of the small party. A woman, both her gray clothing, and her flesh beneath rent, and soaking flowing blood, lay half rested against a stone. Before her crouched either the black hound which had not too long ago menaced them, or else its twin. There were blood flecks in the foam about its jaws yet it did not spring as it was crouched to do. The woman held in a shaking, near falling hand, something from which swung a chain and was glistening with light. Yet for all her struggle she could not continue to hold that steady.

For the moment, forgetting her own horror of that beast, Kelsie stormed in swinging the belt. The stone heavy buckle thudded neatly home on the hound's bony side. It sprang, not at the woman but back, giving tongue in a fearsome cry. Kelsie swung again and this time the very edge of the rock contacted with the side of one forepaw. Again that cry and now the beast turned and fled though it did not go out of sight but ran back and forth as if awaiting reinforcements.

Kelsie backed away, toward the woman.

"Sister—"

The word rang in her head and she dared, for a moment, to look away from the hound to the bleeding survivor of that stricken party. The woman's hand had fallen across her body, but her eyes were still open and fixed on Kelsie with such appeal that the girl dropped down on one knee. As she did that the wildcat moved in closer, ducked its head so that the woman's limp hand lay but a fraction away. To Kelsie's amazement the mouth in that white, pain stricken face drew into the shadow of a smile.

"Sister—in—fur—also—" The words were in her mind.

Kelsie shot a look at the snarling hound, but that had not advanced again.

"I—the—last—gate—" the words formed for her with pause between. Though she did not loose her belt weapon she tried to reach to the body before her. That steady streaming of blood—she *must* do something. As if she had in her turn spoken aloud she saw the woman's head turn the slightest from side to side.

"The—last—gate—" came the mind word which Kelsie had to accept sprang from that limp body. "The jewel—" it was as if the woman had a last spurt of strength, "do—not—let them take it!" With infinite effort she again raised her hand.

It was the cat who darted head forward through the loop of the dangling chain. Straightway the woman loosed her grip on what she held so that a sparkling ovid fell free to dangle against the cat's brindle fur.

"We must get help—" Kelsie for a moment looked wildly around as if she could produce by will alone medical assistance which did not exist.

The smile had not faded.

"Sister—I—am Roylane—" There seemed to be some great significance in that. Then the lean body shuddered and the smile faded. "The—gate—" She who was wounded looked beyond Kelsie at something which the girl, quick to turn, could not see. Then the woman sighed and her head dropped upon one shoulder. Though Kelsie had seldom seen death of her own kind before—just once and that was long ago—she knew that this stranger who spoke without the need for words was gone.

She held the belt between her teeth and straightened out the slight body, shrinking in spite of herself from the blood on her hands. Then she looked at the other bodies. Though the hound paced back and forth before two of them, the third lay closer and one outthrust arm pointed straight toward her still clasping a sword. With one eye ever for the hound Kelsie crossed quickly and freed that weapon from the flaccid fingers, finding it so heavy compared to the fencing foils she had known that she nearly dropped it. But clumsy as she might be with it she took courage from the very heft of that blade—a weapon much better than her belt-and-stone defense.

There was a croaking from beyond. The hound took heart from that, throwing back its head to voice another of the direful howls. At that sound the cat took off in great bounds and was gone back to the safety of the stones. Kelsie hesitated by the body of the woman. But there was nothing she could do for her now and apparently the reinforcements the hound expected were on the way. So she followed, but partially backing so that the evil thing could not jump her, swinging the belt warningly, lifting the sword in her other hand.

It made no move to lengthen its stride as it ran back and forth, nor to come at her. Only it howled and that noise tore at her. Finally she broke and ran.

"The gate—" the dead woman had said. Had she and those others with her been heading for the only gate Kelsie knew, that of the circle beyond? It might have been their gate of safety but somehow she knew that the "last" gate was not made of coarse stones and stood waiting here. No, beyond that lay what no living thing might guess.

She saw that gem the cat now carried so awkwardly about its throat give off glints which might be the sparks of a real fire. Already the animal had joined its family on the coat. Kelsie put on a second burst of speed to join it. Throwing herself down on the sod, the sword falling out of her hold, and gasping for breath, she looked back the way she had come. So far no lean black hound, no rider on a skeleton mount appeared.

Only that this was a land haunted with peril she was firmly convinced. She took up the heavy sword for a second time and examined it. The blade tapered from hilt to point, but not with the thin grace of a rapier. The hilt was plain, with a stiff wire wound around and around it to secure the grip. There was no ornamentation on it at all. She got slowly to her feet and tried a thrust and parry, but this was not a point weapon, she decided, rather one meant to be used with the edge of the blade for the blow and of that kind of fighting she knew nothing at all. Fighting? What did she know of that?

For the second time she turned slowly as if she stood on a pivot surveying all which lay beyond the circle. Had the murdered party beyond that down slope been trying to reach this place when they had been overwhelmed? But—where was *here*? What *had* happened to her? Somehow she could no longer hold onto the tattered story she had been telling herself that this was all hallucination. The "last gate"—did "last" signify that there were other gates which the dying woman had known of? She was facing a gate now—two unworked slabs of stone standing well above her height with a third laid across them. That was a gate—yes, and the one on Ben Blair's flank back there—had that been a gate, too?

Kelsie shivered. There were tales enough told in the Scottish mountains—of people who had gone away and then returned—seemingly having been gone by their own measurement of time for but a night or so, but really for years!

Tales—

She got to her feet and walked toward that gate. There was nothing beyond but stretches of mossed rock, stands of the white bell flowers and the rise of stones which was a screen between them and the dead. If she tried could she go *through*?

She closed her eyes and tried to concentrate on the tumble of stones she had seen for such a short time before she arrived here. They had been in the long summer twilight with the moon hardly giving any help. One had lain so—she remembered that, for the cat had leaped it even as she had struck up Neil's shotgun. And there had been—she held to a badly faded mind picture and took two steps more. She opened her eyes.

Yes, she had ventured out of the shadow of the gate but

she was still in the unknown. Behind her came a warning cry from the cat and she saw the snaky form of the lean hound among the rocks. Kelsie leaped backward into what she had come to consider the only safety in this place of many alarms and death.

The cat snarled. Somehow she had managed to get her neck out of the chain of the jewelry. Now she stood once more before her kits one paw planted flat upon that fiery stone. Kelsie waited alertly for the appearance of a rider, since the first hound had come so attended.

Instead there was a crawling man, striving on hands and knees to come toward her, wavering back and forth. Kelsie's first thought was to run to his aid. But she expected the hound to turn and rend him as he passed and the beast made no such move. It was that which held her in her place.

"Ahhheeee—" surely that cry had come from the crawler. And it was followed by another. If he spoke words there were none that she knew. On impulse she went down on one knee by the cat and reached for the chain but now the cat snarled at her and struck out with its injured paw as if it would flay the skin from her fingers.

"Aaaaahaaaa—" there was no mistaking now that the wounded man crawling toward the circle had thrown back his head and was screaming.

The hound crossed over behind him and was apparently driving him toward the very shelter that he sought. Perhaps the creature had by this some way to force the barrier which had defeated its fellow accompanying the masked rider. If so Kelsie had no mind to see how it would work.

She strode toward the gate with some vague idea of defense in her mind. Thrusting the sword point into the center of a bed of moss so that it stood up close to her hand she stood dangling the once tried and to her more effective measure of the weighted belt.

Now the crawling man was mouthing sounds like frantic words—though they meant nothing to her. Once he crouched, leaning heavily on one arm as he held out his other hand beseechingly in her direction. And, she noted, the hound did nothing to harass him. The creature wanted him in and anything which would serve that one's purpose was to be avoided.

Now he was lower to the ground, drawing himself painfully along by grasping the turf. Between his shoulders an arrow shaft nodded back and forth. Still the hound held off, even withdrew a pace or so.

There came a keening call, Kelsie ducked as a shadow swept over her, looking up at a large black bird, its wing sweep stretched near as far as she was tall. She ducked, thinking that it was seeking her. But it shot up as quickly as it had swooped. Not before she saw that its overlarge eyes were, like those of the rider's mount, pits of swirling, greenish-yellow flame.

Once more it planed down at her. She swung the belt wildly and snatched for the waiting sword, but it stayed just beyond her reach. She heard above the whimpering noise which was now coming from the crawling man, the yowling of the cat, crouched above its helpless kittens.

Whether the purpose of the bird thing would ever have succeeded and driven her out of the circle Kelsie was never to know for there shot through the air a flash of blue light followed by the cracking sound of a whip.

Kelsie, her back now firmly against the rock which helped to support the gate on one side, looked toward that slope down which she had gone to hunt water.

There were two of them, riders. But not like the muffled black one who had tried to reach her before. Their mounts were not horses but shining coated red-cream beasts, each with a horn on its forehead. And the riders—Kelsie blinked and blinked again. Surely now her eyes were playing tricks on her.

When they had first burst into view certainly they had been dark of hair, almost dusky of skin, but now that they were in the full sunlight they showed hair as gilt as true gold and cream skin which their vividly green clothing made all the more fair. There were no reins in their hands, they might have been allowing their striking mounts to range freely.

But each bore what looked like a stock of a whip, and, even as she watched, Kelsie saw the woman draw back her arm and snap out what seemed a line of pure fire, not as visible as a real lash, at the flying thing above.

It squawked raucously and soared well above that flash while the hound gave forth another of its coughing howls. But the crawling man lay supine and unmoving now. Around the circle of the stones pounded the newcomers. The woman leaned over and looked at the body bearing the arrow but she did not dismount nor strive to give any aid.

Her companion wheeled on the hound and it was not as lucky as the flying creature in escape, for the flicking tip of the burning lash the rider wielded struck on its flank and there was a puff of oily smoke. To be followed an instant later by a bursting noise and then the hound was gone, leaving only an oily black deposit on the stones among which it had tried to hide.

The woman's mount paused before the gate and she called aloud, her words unintelligible but clearly aimed at Kelsie, who made a helpless gesture with her free hand, still keeping grip upon her belt weapon.

"I do not understand you," she called back. These riders did not bring with them the miasma of evil which had hung above the other creatures and the black rider. That they meant her no harm she was halfway satisfied. But they were clearly of this world which had changed so much and so— could they really be trusted?

The woman stared at her for a space and now she was joined by the other rider. As his mount came to a halt beside hers Kelsie witnessed again that weird change in the two of them. Their hair changed to a red and there was a golden glint of freckles now across the woman's high-bridged nose. It was as if instead of two riders she faced a number, all contained in a single person. Now the woman no longer spoke, rather she stared straight into Kelsie's eyes, a look of concentration making hers intent and searching.

"Who—" the word was faint and if anything more had

been added to that mind touch Kelsie did not receive it. But it was plain that she had been questioned.

"I am Kelsie McBlair," she spoke slowly, sure that the rider could not understand. Then, with a great effort, she tried something else—pictures out of her memory—of the fallen stones, her struggle with McAdams and her awaking here. She was aware of a yowl from behind her and knew that the wildcat was also answering in its own fashion.

"—gate!" Again Kelsie was sure that she had missed all but one word of something which might be of importance to her.

She nodded, taking the chance that the other meant somehow the archway in which she now stood. The woman rested the stock of her light whip across her mount and with both hands made a series of passes in the air. Where her fingers moved there were left traces of bluish light, not unlike that emitted by the whips, in a complicated design. Seeing that seemed to reassure the spinner of those symbols for she nodded and spoke to the man at her side.

His mount moved back and then he was riding along the trail of blood which had been left by the creeper who lay so flat and silent now. In a moment he had disappeared beyond the rocks toward that scene of death which Kelsie had found earlier.

However, the woman, whose hair had again darkened to near black as there swept a cloud across the sun, slipped from the saddleless back of her mount and approached the girl at the gate. Kelsie kept her tight hold on the belt. She found nothing terrifying about this newcomer but what did she know of anything in this strange and frightening place?

Fur brushed against her leg. The wildcat had come out of the nest she had been so ready to defend. In her mouth gleamed the jewel she had taken from the dying woman, its chain dragging along the ground behind, catching here and there on the flower leaves as she came.

She went forward, out of the stone circle, to drop what she carried at the feet of the woman, who went to one knee caressing the cat with fearless fingers before she caught at the chain and held up the jewel. She did not touch the stone, keeping instead her hold only on the chain. But there was wonderment and then a flicker of anxiety in her expression. Now she looked to Kelsie again.

"Who—" stronger this time, that mind question, yet still but a single word.

"Roylane—" she answered aloud, guessing again at what the full question might have been. And this time she saw the woman's eyes go wide, her mobile features picturing shock.

"Who—?" the mind word came again and now the hand holding that chain swung it so that the gem gleamed in the sun.

"Kelsie—" the girl repeated.

"Kel-Say," this time the woman shaped the word with her lips not her thought— "Kel-Say."

Three

"——with——"

Again the woman gestured, this time summoningly. Her mount moved up beside her and stood waiting. The eyes it fastened on Kelsie were not burning circles of evilly colored fire as she had seen in the hounds' heads and in that of the skeletonlike steed of the black rider—rather a warm brown and—surely there was intelligence in them!

Kelsie guessed once more at what they wished of her—to accompany them. The circle meant safety from what she had seen threatening in this land—that she knew. Dared she obey that invitation—or was it an order? She could not stand against the flame whips of these two were they to drive her.

To gain time she pointed to the body on the ground.

"What about him?" she asked, spacing her words carefully, trying to think her question at the same time.

The answer came sharp and clear.

"Dead!"

She heard the cat mew and looked down. Already the mother's jaws had closed upon the nape of one of the squirming kittens. Lifting her child high the cat advanced toward the gate, plainly ready to go with this stranger even if Kelsie delayed. That made up the girl's mind for her. She went to gather up her coat, the other mewling infant in it, and returned, stooping, offering the bundle to the wildcat. The mother allowed her burden to drop in with its sibling, winding about Kelsie's legs as she went through the gate at last.

Up the slope came the other rider. He carried before him the body of Roylane and passed them, taking his burden on into the circle. No opposition arose to keep him out, but, as he entered, the blue standing stones flared up like candles and a drifting haze spread from one to another of them. He dismounted and lifted down the body which in his hold seemed small and spare. Then he laid it on the ground, choosing, Kelsie was sure, not just by chance, a bed of the white flowers to receive it. From his belt he produced two brilliantly blue feathers, gleaming like those which formed the tails of those birds she had seen earlier. He pushed one into the ground at the head and the other at the feet of the dead woman, standing up and back at last to raise his two hands to his forehead in what appeared to be a salute, while from his companion there came a sing-songed flow of speech which might have been of farewell or invocation.

As he turned to leave, the trails of mist from the stones rolled out into the center of the circle, settling about that small broken body until only their one rippling substance could be seen.

"——Go——"

Again Kelsie was summoned, and since there was little other choice she went. She sat awkwardly on the back of the woman's mount, her arms full of the coat in which squirmed the kittens. The woman caught up the cat in turn and slipped her into the folds Kelsie held. Then, to the girl's surprise, she also put in the jewel. The cat pawed it beneath her own body as she settled with her family, looking up at Kelsie with a hint of a growl as if warning the girl to take care.

They skirted the gully where the stream flowed and the animal under her fell into a swift pace, joined immediately by its companion. They headed southwest, as well as Kelsie could tell from the sun.

As they went it became more and more certain to the girl

that wherever she might be it was no country she had ever seen or heard of. Strange vegetation arose around them and there were things moving in the tall grass of open glades which had no relationship to any animal she knew.

She noted as they went that the man kept behind and sometimes his mount dropped to a slower pace—he might have been a rear guard. Yet they heard no more of the yowling howls from the hounds, nor any other sounds save the calls of the bright winged birds which swung about them as they rode.

Across open land they traveled. Now and then their mounts trotted by long overgrown fields guarded by the tumbled stones of what were once dividing walls. This had the look of a land long deserted.

At last they came to a way which was marked by a scarring of hoof and footprints and undoubtedly was a road, if one might call such a dusty trail a road. The land began to rise on either side and Kelsie could see that they were entering the throat of a valley between two rises which, a little beyond, assumed the height of real mountains.

On the rock walls they passed were carved a series of signs or what might even have been words of an unknown tongue. The woman with whom Kelsie shared this mount pointed with her flame whip as they passed each of these symbol-graven rocks.

There was a scuttling around a large rock where, settled in a squatting position on the crown, was a shape as bizarre as that of the hound and the monstrous beast the black rider had bestridden.

Shorter than a man, this sentinel, for so she would deem him with its spear held up in salute to the riders, was a giant lizard, green-gold of scaled skin. It had a domed head which was nearly human in shape, though the lipless mouth which stretched a third of the way back into the skull and the red tongue which quivered in the air (as if testing a breeze which was not at that moment blowing) were grotesque copies of human features. The woman responded to his salute with a raised hand.

Kelsie was sure that they must have passed other guards during their journey, but that was the only one she had seen. Then at last they reached the mouth of a gully road at the border of a land which made her draw a deep breath.

She had seen strangeness and horror since her first awaking here—wherever *here* might be. Now she looked upon true beauty. The land ahead was brilliantly green with lush growth starred here and there with flowers jewel-like in radiant color. She saw to one side a small herd of animals like the one she now bestrode grazing peacefully. There were also people before and beyond, though none of them appeared to show any interest in the emergence of their own small party.

Down they went—the road now vanished and the hillside covered with velvety grass. Then, for the first time, Kelsie saw houses—the brightness of their roofs betraying them to the eye, for their walls were masses of flowering vine. Had the feathers been plucked from countless flocks of the birds such as escorted them and woven into a thatch it would look like that!

For the first time the inhabitants of the valley looked up. Some gathered in a small group of welcome. A few of them shared the peculiarity of those two who had found her, their color of skin and hair changing as they moved. But the others were closer to the woman she had found dying. They were tall and slender and their hair remained very dark, their skin sun browned yet fair.

Four of those who so waited were men, wearing coats of fine mail which, when they moved, appeared to be as supple as cloth. There were two women, one of whom wore green garments which were no different from those of the one whose beast Kelsie shared. But the other had a long straight robe of gray which brushed the grass with its hem and had a circle of tarnished silver girding it. Her dark hair was drawn severely back and bound into a net also of silver, while her pallid face reminded Kelsie strongly of the woman who had died from the savaging of the hound.

It was she who started forward as they drew up, but her

attention was all for the gem half hidden by one of the cat's paws. Her lips moved, breaking the statue-like stillness of her face, and she stared first at the woman in green and then at Kelsie. It seemed to the latter that there was both suspicion and threat in that long moment of straight regard.

She herself slipped from the back of the sleek mount, her coat with the kittens still held close. But the cat had leaped lightly to the earth the minute they had come to a halt and was now weaving a pattern brushing against the long gray skirt, the chain of the jewel gripped between its teeth.

The woman stooped and drew her fingers across that bushy head and then looked again to Kelsie, speaking in that lilting language. Regretfully the girl shook her head.

"I do not understand—"

Several of those waiting looked startled and the woman in gray frowned. Then in her aching head Kelsie felt once more that troubling sensation:

"—who/—what/—"

For the second time she pictured the scene on the side of Ben Blair, trying to remember every small item. If these people could read minds surely they must be able to pick out an answer from what she spread before them. But the frown on the woman's face only grew sharper and there was a murmur of near whispers speeding from one listener to another.

"——gate——" That had come from the woman who had found her. She now touched Kelsie's arm to attract her full attention and pointed to herself:

"Dahaun." She shaped that name with exaggerated movements of her lips, and once again Kelsie answered:

"Kelsie."

"Kel-Say—" Dahaun nodded, pointed to the woman in gray, and said a word which again Kelsie faithfully repeated. Thus those others were made known to her.

After two tries the girl managed:

"Crytha, Yonan (who looked to be the youngest of the men), Kemoc, Kyllan." And for the one who towered above the rest "Urik."

The cat reared on its hind legs and clawed at Kelsie demandingly. When she put down the coat with its family the mother went to them at once, licking them all over as if she distrusted what might have happened to them during that ride. Kelsie herself was urged on into the nearest of the strange living houses and into an inner part of that where behind curtains there bubbled a shallow pool of water. Dahaun made motions to suggest that she shed her clothing and make use of such refreshment. She began to point hither and thither and give words which Kelsie said after her, striving to use the proper intonation.

By the time she was through with her bath and had toweled herself dry on a square of stuff she had a vocabulary of perhaps twenty-five words which she continued to say over to impress them on her mind.

She ate from a tray loaded down with fruit, nuts, and small cakes, feeling strangely free in the garments Dahaun had provided. There was an under smock of pale green and trousers not unlike rather tight jeans. Then came a long-sleeved jerkin which was laced up the front with cords of silver and belted with links of that same metal embossed and engraved into intricate patterns. On her feet were soft boots, calf high, which fitted fairly well. She was offered a comb to set her short cut locks into order, still being lessoned all the while in the language.

There was a stir outside which even small rustling of the leaves set in the wall above did not hush. At a call from Dahaun a tall man, mail clad, tramped in. He carried his helmet on his hip, showing himself bareheaded and full faced. His was a face to attract interest. The skin was weathered brown as if he had been much in the open, and there were silver streaks in the very dark hair at his temples. His eyes were gray and he looked at Kelsie searchingly almost as if he would open her head if he could, and have out of her answers to questions she did not even know existed.

"You are from the gate—"

Startled, she stared at him openmouthed. He was speaking her own language!

"Gate?" she floundered. "There was no gate—just the stones. Neil knocked me down when I tried to keep him from shooting the cat. I had every right," the almost forgotten heat of her temper was again a trace of warmth in her. "I had posted the land—up to the Lying Stones and beyond. Where . . . where is this?"

She made a small gesture to indicate what lay about them, house, strangers—this land itself.

"You are in the Green Valley," he told her, "in Escore. And you came through one of the Gates— May the Lady turn her favor to you now."

"Who are you?" she came directly to the point, "and what are the gates?"

"For the first, I am Simon Tregarth. And for the second—it would take an adept to make that clear to you— if he or she could."

"How do I get back?" She asked the most important question of all.

He shook his head. "You do not. We have only one adept now and your gate is not his. Even Hilarion cannot send you back."

The woman in gray had entered behind him. Now she pushed to the front though she kept a space between them as if she had some aversion to the man. She addressed him abruptly and he shrugged before he turned again to Kelsie. It was plain that there was little liking between the two of them.

"She who is Wittle would know how you came by that jewel. Surely you did not bring it with you."

"She had it—the woman who died—Roylane."

There was complete silence and they were all staring at her as if she had uttered some word or words which had dire meaning.

"She gave you her name?" countered the man who had called himself Tregarth.

Kelsie's chin went up, she sensed disbelief in that question.

"When she was dying," she returned shortly.

Tregarth turned to the woman in gray and spoke quickly. Though she might be listening to him she never looked away from Kelsie. Something in that unending stare made the girl more and more uneasy, as if in each blink of an eye she was being accused of the death of the traveler and her companions.

However, Tregarth had once more turned his attention full upon the girl.

"Did you also take her jewel, and by her word?"

Kelsie shook her head emphatically, her denial aimed more at that woman in gray than to him. "The cat took it," she said. Let them believe or not it was the truth. And she added to her first statement by describing just how the animal had taken the gem from its owner. Once more she was aware of a brush of thick fur against her and looked down to see the wildcat come to a stop before her, seating itself with tail tip covering both its good foot and the mangled one together, as if it was the two of them against this world.

The woman in gray was plainly startled by the appearance of the cat. The ornament still lay around the animal's neck. The cat dipped its head to catch the gem between its jaws once again.

Though she had started forward a step and uttered a sound as if denying the cat its trophy, the gray woman now stood, plainly completely astounded by the creature's actions.

"This is as it was before?" Tregarth asked.

"Yes. Only the cat took that—" Kelsie thought it wise to make that point as soon as possible. She had no desire to be thought of as one who had robbed the helpless dead. Though why she would want such a bauble she had no idea.

"And the cat entered the gate before you or with you." He did not make a question of that statement. But she saw fit to answer:

"Yes."

Now it was Dahaun who broke in with a fast burst of speech in which Kelsie heard her own name and the word "gate" mentioned several times. First Tregarth and then the gray woman nodded, the latter reluctantly, Kelsie believed. She watched the other bring a small bag out of some hidden pocket in her robe and pull at its drawstring until the pouch lay flat on the mat covered floor. Going down on one knee she spread out the bit of cloth yet more and then turned to the cat, meeting it eye to eye though she uttered no sound.

If she was asking it to give up guardianship of the stone she was unsuccessful. For the cat drew back, though still facing her, until there was more space between them. A line showed between the woman's eyes which looked so pale under her dark brows. She spoke now, something with a certain rhythm which could have been part of a ritual. But the cat did not move. At length she picked up the bag and as she did so shot another keen and threatening look at Kelsie, speaking as one with authority.

Tregarth heard her out and then translated for Kelsie's benefit.

"You are bidden to make your familiar let the power go—"

"Bidden?" snapped Kelsie. "I have no control over the cat. Familiar—" a scrap of old knowledge came suddenly to the fore of her mind, "that's what they used to say about witches—that they had animals to help them. Well, I do not know where your Green Valley is, nor Escore, nor any of this country! I am not a witch—such things do not exist."

For the first time there was a quirk of smile about his lips. "Oh, but here they do, Kelsie McBlair. This is the very home and root of what you might call witchcraft in your own place."

She laughed uncertainly. "This *is* a dream—" she said more to herself than him.

"No dream," his voice was entirely serious and, Kelsie thought, he was looking at her with something close to pity. "The gate is behind you and there is no going back—"

She threw up her hands. "What is all this talk of gates?" she demanded. "I'm probably back in a hospital somewhere and this is all coming from that bump on the head—" But, even as she tried to hearten herself with that thought and speech, she knew that it was not the truth. Something far past her ability to answer with anything believable had happened.

The woman in gray advanced another step, now her hand came out palm up to Kelsie and her frown grew the darker. She exploded into a burst of words which ran up the scale of sound near to a command shout.

"She is the witch!" Kelsie counterattacked.

"Yes," Tregarth answered calmly and with a certainty which made it the truth. "Have you any control over the cat?"

Kelsie shook her head vigorously. "I told you she took the thing from that woman—that Roylane, when she was dying and the woman let her. It was not given to me. Let this—this *witch* beg it from the cat."

Tregarth was already studying the animal, now he turned to the one who had brought Kelsie here. He asked her a question in that other tongue which sounded almost like the twittering of excited birds. It was Dahaun's turn to face the cat, taking the disputed stone away from the self-proclaimed witch and moving it nearer her own hand.

For a long breath or two they all stood waiting, Kelsie was plagued by the thought that the cat understood all that had passed and was content now to tease them. Then at last the animal dropped her head to spit the stone straight before her into the center of a piece of shimmery cloth which the woman of the riders had produced. The witch moved but Dahaun waved her back. It was she who drew the cords to make a bag and then held that by the drawstring.

"For the shrine—" Tregarth spoke to Kelsie. "Its power has died with she who held it." Then Dahaun arose, leaving the bag on the ground where the cat caught it up by the string, and spoke to the witch whose pallid face was a little flushed now and whose mouth was a straight line of severity. She turned quickly, her gray robe spinning out at her momentum and went, all those gathered there allowing her wide room.

Tregarth watched her go and now it was his turn to frown. Once more he spoke to Kelsie.

"She is not in agreement with this. Stay away from her until she accepts the fact that her sister-in-power really did as you and Swiftfoot have said," he gestured to the cat. "They have ruled too long, those of Estcarp, to take easily being thwarted, even in small things. And she had counted much on the coming of her sister-in-power. That one died—how?"

The "how" came with a snap of a whiplash. Kelsie told of the arrows she had seen which had cut down the guards and the hound which had attacked the woman.

"There was little to be seen, though," she said and he was as quick to seize upon that:

"Rider?"

She told of him who had besieged her in the circle and Tregarth's hand went to the hilt of the sword he wore, his lips drawn tight in a grimace which was far from a smile.

"Sarn! Sarn riders—and so close—" his words changed to the chirping speech of the Valley people and she caught one now and then which she understood—such as "near," "stone," and "gate."

Dahaun suddenly reached out and took Kelsie's hands before the girl could move or draw back. She nodded abruptly to one of her own people, who produced a dagger in the hilt of which was set a piece of glittering blue metal, akin in color to the stones behind which the girl had sheltered. He passed it across Kelsie's upturned palms, not touching her flesh but close enough so that she felt warmth as the metal seemed to blaze up for an instant. Then, with her eyes still on Kelsie, Dahaun's face became a mask of concentration.

Some of the old pain awoke in the girl's head. But there was more too—not words but thoughts—thoughts not of her own.

"You are—summoned one. Foretold—"

She was not getting the whole message, she knew, but those words made her blink. Summoned—she had been brought here, yes, but not called—unless their quick bearing of her away from the circle could be termed that. Foretold—more of this witchcraft business, that was what that seemed to mean. She spoke to Tregarth:

"I was not summoned—and how—"

Now she was sure there was a note of sympathy in his voice as he answered her.

"The gates open by powers we do not understand. That you came through one unused for generations is enough to single you out as one of importance. This is a land torn by war—Light against the Dark. It is easy to believe for those of us who have faced much which is outside ordinary experience to say that you were summoned. And it was foretold in the last scrying that one would come—"

"I don't know what you mean! I don't care! If there *IS* a gate let me go back—" she cried out then.

He shook his head. "The gates open but once, except when an adept lays a geas upon them. There is no going back."

Kelsie stared at him and within her a chill spread outward from the very center of who and what she was.

Four

There had passed two nights and this was the third day. Kelsie climbed from the green bowl of the Valley into its guardian heights and crouched in a huddle between two rocks facing that stretch of the unknown. She had to force herself to accept what Simon Tregarth had told her, that she and the wildcat had come through some mysterious gate in time and space to another world—and, as far as Simon knew, there was no going back. She was not ready to accept the rest of it—that she had been somehow summoned or kidnapped and brought by the Gate to answer some need here. It was far easier to accept that chance had entrapped her.

If there was no going back then it was best that she prepare herself for this country. She worked hard at the lilting tongue of the Green Silences people, even picked up words from the other race who shared this outpost of safety, for such Tregarth assured her that the Valley was. It was only because she had been able to pass by certain symbols when they brought her here that she was judged to be worthy of the refuge at all. Even then she had been closely questioned concerning both the black rider and the dying witch several times over.

That other witch—the cold gray pillar frightened her more than anyone she had met—even the Rider and his hound. Mainly, Kelsie thought, it was because the woman was here on equal terms and could influence minds against her if she so chose. That was a chance she would be likely to take on the first sign of any weakening on the part of Dahaun and her people. Kelsie avoided her with determination though she believed that twice at least that other had made an effort to approach her.

Thoughts—or were they threats in the form of thought?— had crawled along the edges of her mind and she had fought them fiercely. She had discovered that fixing her attention full upon some object and concentrating intently seemed to baffle that crawling, creeping invasion of her mind. Twice she had been driven to inner battle to defend herself, both times when Dahaun and Tregarth were not there, nor even the gray woman so far as she could tell—only that pressure in her mind. Both times she had been able to banish such a ravishment of her inner self by thinking of the dying witch, by saying the name which had passed between them as a kind of talisman of protection.

Each time she had detected that pressure she sensed that the impotent anger grew colder and more menacing. At least the other had not obtained the jewel which seemed her great desire. For the wildcat had taken it to the small lair Dahaun had caused to be made for her and her kittens, and she had not brought the gem into the light again.

Resolutely now Kelsie began again to turn over and examine the facts she had learned. Not all within this place of safety were even of human form—yet they all appeared to share intelligence and a common purpose.

There were those who went armed like Tregarth and others of his kind, both men and women. There were the people of Dahaun whose ever-changing color seemed to draw strength from the belts and arm bands they wore. These were made of bright blue-green gems which might have life—of a kind.

There were the lizard folk, golden-green with crested heads and eyes as hard as gems, who skittered in and out among the rest or sat at ease playing games with small brilliantly colored pebbles. With them were the Renthans—those tireless beasts, one of whom she had ridden hither. And there were airborne creatures even more strange.

Those she had learned to call the flannen—tiny humanoid bodies supported by dazzling iridescent wings. To watch them dance in the air brought more astonishment than many of the other wonders. Then there were giant birds, or creatures which had the appearance of birds, who cruised the air in regular flights as if they would keep off some danger aimed from the heights. For, for all its assured safety, this Valley and those it held were under siege.

Twice she had seen parties of sentries depart from or go up into the heights and once there had been a wounded man among those returning. Each night there was a great fire in the open space beside the river which was a loose coil of silver ribbon in the land. And into that Dahaun's people tossed in solemn ritual certain bundles of leaves and faggots of sticks so that the light smoke which arose was scented with spicy odors.

"Kel-say—"

She started. Under one of the soft boots she wore a stone loosened and rolled.

Not Dahaun, nor Tregarth, but she whom Kelsie had taken the greatest pains to avoid—the gray woman. Now she seated herself composedly on a well-chosen rock where Kelsie could not get away without actually brushing past her.

"You are very brave—or very foolish—" The woman might have been as at home in speaking the language as Tregarth—or else by some power she had opened knowledge for the girl she faced, "to give your name so openly. Do you not believe then in your own place that a name is the proper label of a being? Or are you so well protected that you need have no fears? What craft do you practice there, Kel-Say?"

There was a mocking note in her voice and Kelsie was

quick to define it. Her resentment for that moment was greater than the uneasiness and wary fear this one always aroused in her.

"I practice no craft," she returned sullenly. "I do not know why I am here and your gate—" she drew a deep breath.

The witch shook her head. "Not *my* gate—we meddle not in such matters—though once," she sat very straight and there was a shadow of pride on her face, "we could do much which perhaps rivaled the secrets of the gates. But—" did her square shoulders slump a little now under the heavy folds of her gray overmantle? "that time is past. Tell me, girl—Kel-Say," again she drawled out that name, mouthing it as if she said something momentous, "who rules the craft in your place and time?"

"If you mean witches," Kelsie flashed hotly in return, "there are none—really. It is all just stories— Oh, some people dabble with old beliefs and talk about the moon, have ceremonies which they swear have come down from the old times—but it is all just their imaginations!"

There was silence between them and again Kelsie felt that probing within her head as if the other tested her for some shield.

"You believe what you have just said." The woman's stare changed from challenge to wonder. "You believe! How did matters go awry then in your time that the true knowledge was so lost? Yet Tregarth," it seemed to Kelsie that she spoke that name with a lip twist of disgust, "has a measure of the power and he says that he is from your world—by another gate."

Kelsie pulled herself up to sit on a rock so that they were face to face, the woman not looking down at her.

"I do not know what you mean by power—" But was that the truth? There had been the besieging of the circle and certainly the Rider had used no normal weapon to try to get at her, nor had he been able to force his mount into that circle of stones, yet she could pass easily out and back.

"See? You do—at least power as it is here and now." The other might well have reached within and read her thoughts. "The scrying said one would come and it would mean portentous things. And Roylane," again her mouth twisted as if she found it very difficult to say that name, "yielded up her jewel—"

"Not to me," Kelsie pointed out.

"Ah, yes. The cat. And what is the meaning of that, Kel-Say? Answer me now with the truth." She raised one hand and snapped her fingers. A flash of blue light sped toward the girl and Kelsie ducked. Not soon enough—the spark touched her temple and it was as if a ball of fire had broken apart inside her head. She screamed and swayed.

"Arkwraka!"

Kelsie, still swaying, saw another lash of fire come apparently from the sky, cutting between her and the witch. A man, one of Dahaun's people, raised his arm again and a second lash of fire, for she could feel the very heat of it, passed before her but not aimed at either her or the witch.

He who had used the flame whip advanced another step or so and Kelsie recognized him as Ethutur, the co-ruler with Dahaun of this place of peace, while at his shoulder, keeping step with him, though he carried no bared weapon, was the young man Kelsie had had named to her as Yonan, one of the scouts who went beyond the limits of the Valley and dared the evil at its blackest.

"You call on no such tricks here," Ethutur spoke directly to the witch and her previously calm face now was drawn up into a snarl.

Her lips moved as if she would spit like an enraged cat. But when she answered her voice was even enough.

"This one is no kin of yours—"

"Nor of your blood either," he returned. "If she gives anything she will give it openly and by her own consent. This is a place of freedom—there is no mistress, no servant here—"

"You are all servants!" flared the witch.

"To a greater Power than you or anyone else within this Valley can call upon!"

"The Dark has penetrated many places where the Light says or once said that it holds rule. Even your oath-bound Lady does not know for sure what she has welcomed into the heart of her safe land. Those who come through the gates have gifts, talents, compulsions that none of us can name. I would learn more from this one—that she not be the key by which the Dark can open *your* gate!"

"Your rule runs over mountain—or it did, Wise One. But it would seem that you cannot now summon any quorum of your sisters to do much more than the Wisewomen who follow the Lady can. You came to us of Escore for aid for your losses and now you go your own bold way and do not abide by the bounds laid upon power here. You know well that the use of one power always awakens the Dark and in a way strengthens it by that arousing. I say to you now—go your own way or that shall not run with ours!"

"You are a man!" Now there were flecks of spittle shot forth from her lips, an unusual flush painted her sharp cheekbones. "What do you know of Power save through such toys as that!" she gestured to the whipstock he still held. "The higher power—"

"Is for any who can hold it—man or woman," he said. "We follow not your ways of Estcarp here. There are those to be named who wrought mightily in the old days and who were also men. Boast not too loudly of your sistership, seeing to what it has been reduced."

"To save our world!" Her flush was fading but her eyes were wells of anger and Kelsie could feel that emotion, or believed she could, issuing forth from that spare, gray-cloaked body.

"To save your world," he nodded. "Well you wrought for your people. But again I say your ways are not ours and under our sky remember that."

He spoke with none of the emphasis which anger had given her words but she was still wrapped in a red rage as she turned and walked away from them. And Ethutur did not turn to see her go, as if she had already been put out of mind. He spoke now to Kelsie:

"You would do well to avoid that one. She brings with her all the narrowness of the west and I think that she will be a long time giving way to another way of life. It is true that the witches of Estcarp wrought mightily to defend their land against two different evils, but in their last battle they not only exhausted their realm of power but they also lost many of their number, drained of life itself. Now they come questing here for a renewal of what they lost—not only power for those still alive within their citadel but also for those with talent whom they may take and train in their own ways of life. And I do not think, Lady, that you would find what they have to offer good—"

"She came to me," protested Kelsie, "not I to her. I want nothing more from her. And this power of which so much has been said, I do not know or want it."

Ethutur shook his head slowly. "In life it is not what we want which balances our scales—rather it is what the Greater Ones have seen fit to give us at our birth hour. There can be that locked within a man—or a woman—which such do not know that they bear and which comes forth at a time of stress unsummoned. Once awakened that can be trained as any weapon is mastered by one who wishes to wield it." Now he smiled and pointed to the young man still a pace or so behind him. "Ask of Yonan what he found to be his portion."

But Yonan did not match that smile. Instead his face remained in somber lines as if he saw little that was lighthearted in his world.

"Unasked for," he said as Ethutur paused, "To so gain anything one walks a hard road. But—" he shrugged, "we come to you, Lady, to ask where walks that furred one who came with you through your gate."

"I don't know," Kelsie was surprised at his change of subject and the young man must have read that in her expression for he added:

"There is reason." Yonan had been carrying one arm

close to his chest, the bulk of a cloth wrapped loosely around it. Now he held it out to her and there sounded a thin mewling cry. The movement disturbed the wrapping of the cloth and she saw a small white furred head upheld, blind eyes fast shut, and a mouth open for another cry.

"The gray ones," Yonan's voice was harsh, "cornered a snow cat and had their pleasure with her and one cub. This one Tsali found and rescued. It will die if it cannot be fed."

"But it is so big," Kelsie was already reaching out for the well-wrapped cub. "It must be as big as both of the kittens—and the wildcat—"

"Swiftfoot," he corrected her and she looked at him amazed.

"Have you already named her then?"

"She named herself to the Lady of Green Silences. All which run, fly or swim, and are not of the shadows, are friends to the Lady. But the cubling will die—"

"No!" The weaving of that blindly seeking head, the small wail of hunger and loneliness brought Kelsie out of the preoccupation with herself and the anger of the witch to the here and now. "She took her kittens to a place of her own yesterday. I have not seen her save when she came to feed."

As he relinquished the weight of the cub into her arms she knew that she must indeed find her fellow wayfarer and see if Swiftfoot would accept a fosterling. Some cats did so readily as she well knew.

Surely the wildcat had found a lair somewhere along the gashed cliffs which sheltered the Valley. Their many shallow caves and cracks would attract her—and it could not be too far from the living houses as the cat had easily come morning and evening for her own nourishment.

Kelsie gathered the bundled creature to her and then looked to Yonan.

"What is this?"

"Snow cat," he repeated shortly. "The mother must have

been hunted well out of the mountains to come so far afield. The gray ones are roaming afar when they fasten on such prey."

The cub was nuzzling her fingers, sucking hungrily, halting now and then to whimper its need. Resolutely Kelsie turned her back on the gathering of houses and the tents of the people who were not Valley born and headed for the cliff side. As she went she began to call—not the "kitty-kitty" of her own time and place but with her mind. Before that moment she had not thought of trying to do that. It was easy enough to picture the wildcat and her kittens, to hold to that picture and keep on summoning, in a way she could not have put words to, that unsought companion in her adventure.

She was aware that Yonan followed her, but some distance behind as if he feared in some way to confuse her searching. They scrambled over several falls of rock and past one stream which bored through the hills to find its path to the river. Then Kelsie stopped short.

It was as if a new sense had been added to the five she had carried so far through life. This was not scent, sight, nor hearing, but it was touch of a different kind. As she concentrated upon it the wildcat came into sight around the side of a large boulder, one of those on which ancient carvings had been so weathered that only traces of their pattern could be sighted. Kelsie took a step toward her and Swiftfoot's lips drew back in a warning snarl. Though the girl had carried both the cat and her kittens on their journey to the Valley, Swiftfoot was announcing that this had been only a temporary measure and she would allow no more such liberties. What had they said back beyond the Gate, that no one could tame a true wildcat? It would seem that such warnings were right.

Kelsie went no farther. Instead she juggled the wrapped cub to one hip and braced herself against the ancient work to come to her knees at its foot. Then she settled the cloth on the ground before her and pulled away its folds so that the hungry and now continually wailing cub was wholly revealed.

She carefully kept her thoughts to herself. Even if she could think Swiftfoot into coming to examine this newcomer she would not dare to try. She knew too little about this new force she had tapped to try to use it further.

The cub continued to wail. Swiftfoot snarled and then her slitted eyes turned toward the youngling. Slowly, only an inch at a time as she might have advanced upon some prey, she came forward, belly low to the gravel, stopping now and again to eye Kelsie who held herself stiffly quiet, waiting.

Perhaps the cub scented something of its near kin for now its head swung toward the cat, though its eyes could not see, and its wail reached a higher pitch. The cat sprang and Kelsie flung out one arm fearing that death rather than life for the cub was the result of her experiment.

Swiftfoot crouched over the cub which was perhaps a fourth of her own size. Her tongue flicked forward and licked the blind head. Then she sought to grip the loose rolls of skin at its neck, to carry it as she might one of her own kittens. It was almost too great a task for her. The cub bumped along the ground, still wailing, as they disappeared from sight behind the rock. Kelsie turned and saw Yonan some distance from her watching intently.

"She will accept it, I think," the girl said. "But whether it can survive—that no one can promise."

For the first time she saw a shadow on his serious face—a shadow which might serve for a smile.

"It will be well," he seemed very sure. "This is a place of life, not death."

Kelsie thought of all she did not know about the Valley, about these people, of all which she must learn. Must learn? Again that thought thudded home. All Tregarth's talk of gates and how one passed by a single way through them, how much was true? Perhaps all the asking in the world would not tell her that. But what she could learn—that she would.

"You are not of the Valley people," she stated that as a fact not a question. There were truly two humanoid peoples within the Valley—to say nothing of those who were winged, pawed, hoofed, or scaled.

"No," he dropped down facing her, sitting cross-legged, the rumpled cloth in which he had carried the cub lying in a heap between them. "I am of Karston kin—also of the Sulcar—"

He must have seen from her expression that neither word meant anything to her for he launched into more speech than she had heard since Simon Tregarth had ridden out a day earlier.

"We are of the Old Blood—from the south—or my mother was. And when they drove us out because we were what we were we came into the mountain borderlands and took service against the Kolder and those who put our kinsmen to the death. Then when the witches turned the mountain—"

"Turned the mountains!" Kelsie broke in. Maybe she could accept some things but the turning of mountains was not among them.

"All those who ruled in Estcarp," he continued, "they gathered their power so it was as if it were wielded by one alone, and that they threw against the earth itself, so that the mountains tumbled and arose anew, and no man could recognize the border thereafter."

It was perfectly plain that he believed every word he was saying no matter how impossible the feat he described.

"Then," he was continuing, "we sought land of our own and Kyllan Tregarth came to lead us into the older homeland, even this Escore. But there was ancient evil here and it awoke at the coming of the Tregarths for their sister Kaththea is a notable witch, though she wears no jewel, and, what she did in ignorance troubled the land. So once more we war and against a host of Darkness which is more than men such as we faced before. Strange indeed are some of our battles—" He glanced down at his own hand where it rested upon the hilt of his sword. She remembered then that these men who went mail clad were different from the changeable people and seemed often to have hand close to some weapon or another as if they expected nothing but war and alarms as a way of life.

"Who is Simon Tregarth—you speak of Kyllan—"

"Simon is one who came through a gate—even as you, Lady. He was great in the councils of Estcarp when they went against the Kolder and has but recently returned from another venture which took him beyond the accounting of men. He is wed to the Once-Witch Jaelith and sired Kyllan, Kemoc and Kaththea all at one birth. That was a marvel unknown before—the warrior, the warlock, and the witch— and all have done great things in this land.

"But there is still much to be accomplished here. Also there are many things which a man cannot understand—" he was frowning again and running his fingers around the hilt of his sword, even drawing it a fraction once and then slapping it back into the scabbard.

"And some such have happened to you," Kelsie encouraged him when he fell silent, wishing to store away in her memory as much as she could of this place and all there was to do with it. That she was caught here at least for now she could no longer deny. So the more she knew the better it would be for her in days to come. Though what part she could play in such affairs she could not see, nor did she wish to speculate.

"Such happened to me," Yonan agreed. "For a space we have believed that we have beaten back the shadow and that it sulks in its own fastnesses. But you have told us of a Sarn Rider who has dared to come this near to the Valley and deal death to one who should have been mightier than he—"

"Roylane?"

It seemed to Kelsie that he winced as she repeated that name.

"A witch has no name. To give one's name among them gives them power over another. Yet she said her name to you and her stone came with the cat. Thus another change—"

Now she looked at him squarely, catching his eyes and holding them in a way she had never tried with anyone before—as if she could compel him to answer even against his will.

"What do you think I am?"

It was a matter of four or five slow breaths before he answered and then he said:

"You were summoned—the Lady Dahaun had the foreseeing of that. And none can come so unless there is a geas laid upon them—"

"A geas?" she demanded.

"A fated journey or deed against which nothing nor no one can stand. Yes, we knew that one would come—and perhaps *they* did also or a Sarn Rider would not have dared the inner hills. What your geas is—that you will discover for yourself, Lady—"

"You are right about that," she returned grimly, forced against her will into at least half belief.

Five

Kelsie arose abruptly, turning to the rock in which those weird spirals and indentations were plain as the sun moved.

"I know nothing of this . . . this geas—"

He shrugged. "Sometimes that is so and you will find that it leads you only after many days— But where it points, there you shall go."

"You speak as if you know something of such things beside just idle tales."

Yonan again looked at her with the shadow smile. "Now that is also the truth. It once fell upon me—this need for doing an action which I did not plan and—"

Whatever he might have added came to nothing, for one of the lizard folk flashed into sight among the rocks. Yonan was instantly on his feet, staring upward at that green-gold scaled body as it descended the Valley wall with a speed which made Kelsie gasp so near was it to a downward plunge. The girl saw that while using all four limbs for his quick drop the sentry carried in addition something in his mouth, an untidy bunch much the same as the cloth in which Yonan had brought the cub and she wondered if another was to be added to Swiftfoot's family.

Once the lizard reached relatively level ground where the two stood he spat forth what he carried and it slammed against the stone of the carving. There came a tingling sound and then a puff of black smoke accompanied by a foul odor. Yonan exclaimed, drew sword while the lizard man stood, panting to one side, his golden, black slitted eyes on the man.

The tip of the sword caught in the covering of that untidy package, flipped part of the covering up and back. The smoke had disappeared but the odor was stronger, seeming to poison the very air about them.

Under the flap of the material Yonan had lifted there lay a short rod, perhaps the length of one of the lizard man's long-fingered hands. It was a murky grayish color and there was a knob at either end. Plainly it was hollow and a smoky substance within appeared to swirl and billow as if it fought for freedom.

Moving with what appeared exaggerated care Yonan rolled it out of the cloth. By the expression on his face he was as puzzled as the girl as to what this might be. Though she knew from her instant reaction to it that she would not have laid her bare hand upon that artifact, even had she been offered free passage back through the gate. Her quick, nauseated reaction puzzled as well as alarmed her.

There was something like a far off fluttering of speech within her head and then the lizard was gone, running at top speed toward the houses closer to the river, leaving his find under the sword point of Yonan.

"Tsali goes for help—" the young man said. "He must have found this in the rocks above on the very rim of the Valley."

"Look!" Kelsie may not have wanted to touch the stone but she clutched in her growing uneasiness at Yonan's arm.

For that thing on the ground was moving!

Not from any stirring of the sword point. In fact it looked as if it were somehow veering left to escape touch with the steel. As if it were a sentient creature with a will to escape—escape or attack?

This was near to the same anger she had felt when the

Witch Woman had turned against her. There was a will here, somehow clipped within, or acting from a distance without, upon that rod. It had turned enough now to be wholly clear of the cloth and she saw that the knob end coming around to face them was fashioned in the likeness of a head—a grotesque travesty of a human head in which eye slits boiled with the same evil yellow fire she had seen in pits of the hounds' narrow skulls.

To her surprise Yonan reversed his sword in one swift movement and held toward that rolling thing the hilt instead of the point. There came a blaze of blue haze from the pommel of the weapon. It touched the rolling rod and—

That solid looking thing quivered as if it were indeed endowed with life. Also it would appear that Yonan's quick action baffled it though it raised the head end a fraction and wavered for an instant back and forth.

"What is it?" demanded Kelsie. "Is it alive?"

"I have never seen its like before," returned her companion. "But it is of the Dark—the Deepest Shadow perhaps."

Before the words were barely out of his mouth there came a yowl of rage. One she had certainly heard before. Around the rock padded the cat, dragging behind it something which flashed with fiery light. The chain of the witch's jewel dripped from between those cruel fangs and the gem itself boiled and throbbed as if it, too, had a new kind of life within. The cat made a wide circle about that which still quivered and fought for its freedom where Yonan held it in balk.

Padding straight to Kelsie, Swiftfoot dropped the chain of the jewel over the toe of her soft boot and, looking up into the girl's face, gave a second demanding yowl.

The girl bent and scrabbled for the chain which had fallen into the gravel and arose with the sparkling gem twirled only inches from her hand, nearly crying out from the heat the thing was generating.

Now the rod went into a frenzy, rolling back and forth,

but Yonan was watchful and his sword hilt blocked any swing right or left which might take it even temporarily out of the ward that weapon kept upon it.

"Fool!"

It was the Witch Woman's biting voice which led Kelsie to glance back over her shoulder. Her skirt caught up with both hands, the woman out of Estcarp was actually running, outpacing in this instant Dahaun and behind her two others, one in the mail of the Old Race, the other, whipstock steady, a girl of the Valley. But before the three of them came Tsali with a whir of speed.

"Fool!" The witch was panting a little but she arrived first and had strength enough left to swipe outward at Kelsie's hand, as if she would wrest the jewel stone from her then and there. "Would you burn out the last of life—"

"Or the first," Dahaun's voice was much more collected. "What mischief has Tsali discovered within our borders?" She came closer to that trembling, fighting rod, dropping down to view the thing the closer. They were all silent now waiting for her to judge. But at last she shook her head.

"Never has the Valley had its ancient safeguards broken. Yet Tsali found this rolling between rocks and about to fall into the spring, perhaps to let the water hide and bring it down. It is not of the Sarn, nor the gray ones, and certainly not of the Thas—or if so it is something they have never turned against us before. This is very old—and—"

"And," for the first time the man in mail spoke. Kelsie thought at first he was Simon returned. But the face half seen below the helm's nose guard was that of a much younger man. "And, what does that argue, Lady? That those of the Dark have broached some place of ancient weaponry?" He held no sword, rather what seemed a flimsy stick peeled of its bark and with half of its length colored the green-blue of the bird feathers which roofed the Valley houses.

"Well enough," he said to Yonan, "let us see what the Valley can raise against this."

Obediently Yonan stepped away and withdrew his sword hilt from the weaving pattern before the strange thing.

The other man spoke. The single word he uttered held no meaning for Kelsie but once more, as she had shrunk from the powers the witch had called upon her, so again her head was instantly filled with a roaring sound as if the very air about them had been ruptured, letting in she knew not what.

The green half of the wand the man held burst into real flame and with an exclamation, he threw it from him at that rod. It fell into the tangle of cloth and smoldered, beginning a fire which seemed to excite the rod for it rolled deliberately toward that piece of scorching fabric and thrust the head end into the small flame. It might have been feeding greedily on the fast dying spark.

"Ha," the Witch Woman flung back her head and actually uttered a bark of laughter. "See what you would do, Kemoc halfling? This is not for such as you no matter what knowledge you dabbled in in Lormt. Get you off before you make bad matters worse. See—it feeds upon that very thing you would use to quiet it!"

The swirling within the rod part of the lizard man's find did indeed appear to gather strength, and the murkiness was, Kelsie thought, taking on a glow. There was a sudden sharp pain in her hand and she looked to see that the gem was also awhirl at the end of its chain and the links of the chain were sawing at her flesh.

"By Reith and Nieve—" was that her own voice? Whence had come those names? From her lips right enough, but they had not been generated by any thought of hers!

The twirling stone was throwing off sparks, though none reached as far as the object on the ground. She discovered she could not stop the motion of her wrist which controlled that passage through the air.

"No!" Again the Witch Woman gave tongue and she aimed a blow straight at Kelsie's arm. Only Yonan's left hand intercepted that and she was forced a little backward by his abrupt rebuttal to the stroke she tried to deliver.

"She is no witch!" The voice reached a screech. "She dare not use the power. Would you have that which waits fall upon us all? Stop her!" The Witch Woman looked to Dahaun who had made no move either at the destruction of the wand or at the witch's foiled attack on Kelsie. But now she spoke.

"We do not give names—those are given to us. She was given a name and perhaps more by one of your own kin—"

"Who is dead!" That sounded as if the witch thought such an ending might have been well deserved.

"Who is dead," Dahaun agreed. "But in dying she may have passed—"

"There is no likelihood of that," cried the witch. "She has no right—she could not have done so. This one comes from where? She is not of the blood, she has no training, she is nothing except a danger to all of us. Give me the jewel!" Her demand was aimed at Kelsie who had just made a discovery of her own.

Just as she could not stop the twirling of her wrist which kept the gem in motion, so she could not now loose her grip upon it. Instead she was pulled forward as if someone tugged at her with greater strength than she could sustain. The witch gem swung faster, though its circle was wider until it seemed to rest upon the air itself a distance beyond the circumference of that rod.

All the while the rod flapped up and down, strove to roll and could not, as if it did indeed hold life within it. The whir of the jewel grew faster until Kelsie's wrist seemed to be the center of a brilliant disc and the sparks it flung off now shot at the thing on the half-burned cloth.

Again Kelsie's lips shaped words she did not understand:

"Reith—Reith—by the Fire of Reith—by the will of Nieve may this be rendered harmless!"

Wider and more accurate became the rain of sparks. Now they centered straight upon the rod. Then there was a burst of glaring light, first an angry threatening crimson, then blue above and nothing below save a twisted piece of what looked like half-melted metal.

Kelsie's arm fell to her side without her willing it. It was numb as if she had lifted some great weight and held it out for a time past her own strength. The glitter from the jewel had vanished—it was an ashy gray, like a piece from the fire which had burned itself out.

Dahaun broke the silence first. "It is gone—the evil of it."

"Back to the sender," the witch's harsh voice sounded no relief. "And what message will it carry so? That we have come seeking and are ready to stand with you—"

"Seeking you did come," Kemoc reminded her. "But it was not to cast your lot and power with us—you thought to take, not to share."

"Be silent, halfling who should never have been born," her harshness close to hoarseness as if she would scream at him but did not have the power.

"Halfling I may be," he told her, "but that half blood has wrought well for Escore. And before that for Estcarp—"

"Man!" she spat at him. "It is against all nature that a man has the power. Because your sire brought that with him through the gate—what has happened?"

"Yes, what has happened," he returned. "The Kolders are no more, the way to Escore lies open—"

"Which is no blessing," she interrupted. "Things from the foul Dark roam the mountains now and venture down upon the land. You and those two who share birthday with you have stirred into being a mighty stew of war, disaster and death. And now—" she pointed straight to Kelsie who was trying to rub life back into her numb arm, "there comes this one who took from one of the sisters—stole—what she does not know how to handle and so—"

"And so," Dahaun's voice cut clear and cold through that

tirade, "and so this thing whose like we have not seen before has been rendered harmless." She spoke to Kemoc and the girl of her own people. "Let it be buried where it lies and then do you," she motioned to the stone in which the ancient carvings were still to be half seen, "set this upon it. Reith and Nieve," she went to Kelsie and laid her hand protectively on that numbed arm. From her touch came a surge of warmth and the girl discovered she could flex her fingers. "Long and very long has it been since those names were called upon—though they were mighty weapons in their day. Do you still have a touch with them?" she asked the witch.

The latter looked around at the rest of them with both anger and contempt in her face, stronger yet in her voice as she answered:

"Such things are not for talking on—they are secrets—"

Dahaun shook her head. "The time for secrets is long past. When the Dark arises, then the Light must stand united and all knowledge be shared from one to another."

The witch answered her with what sounded like an exclamation of contempt. However, if she would have denied Dahaun's suggestion she did not do so more openly. Instead she gestured toward the now dead looking stone which still dangled from the chain wound about Kelsie's fingers.

"That is of our magic not of yours. It should have been left to rest with her who first gained it. Not given to one who has none of the proper training. How do we know what she is, in truth?"

There was no mistaking the anger which still bubbled in her whenever she glanced at Kelsie. The girl was swift to reply. With the fingers of her left hand she plucked at the chain until it did unwrap from that tight hold and she offered to give it to the witch, only too glad to be free of it, but the woman in gray made a gesture repulsing it, seeming almost to shrink as it came near her.

"Take it," Kelsie urged. "I do not want it—"

"You have no right—" began the witch making no move to accept the stone.

"She has the right of death-gift," Dahaun said. "Did not she who died give also of her name to Kel-Say. And with the name might have gone her power."

"She also had no right!"

"Then call her up and ask her of—"

The flush was high on the angular face of the woman in gray. "That is foulness which you suggest! We have no dealings with such darkness."

"If that is so, why question what your sister has done?" Dahaun asked. "One can pass the power willingly and she did—"

"To a cat!" sputtered the witch. "It was that beast who carried the seeing stone."

"And in a time of need passed it again to one it judged would use it—"

Kelsie was tired of this wrangling over what she might have done or what she might be. She tossed the jewel from her, though she had to use all her willpower to achieve that. For it seemed that her body was a traitor to her mind and would not let it go. It arched through the air, struck upon one of the tall rocks and then slid down into the coarse grass clump at the foot of the stone.

"Take it!" Kelsie had never heard such a note in Dahaun's voice before. Thus in spite of all her defiance and desire to be free of their quarrels she found herself moving forward, her fingers reaching down to a loop of the chain caught about a stiff blade of grass. Once more she held the stone. It was still opaque, showing a muddy gray, and she began to believe that it had burned itself out of whatever mysterious "power" it had shown while confronting the rod. She swung it a little as one might swing a smoldering branch to brighten fire again, but there was no answer from that lump of crystal.

"Give her the covering," now Dahaun had turned that demand upon the witch, her anger plain to read in every stiff gesture brought out that patch of cloth which could be drawn into a bag and smoothed it out on top of one of the stones.

Thankfully Kelsie loosed the chain and let the jewel fall onto that circle releasing her hold. The witch had drawn the drawstrings the minute she placed it so and stepped away, leaving the knobby bag on the rock's crown.

"Take it—" Dahaun ordered.

Kelsie dared to shake her head. "I do not want it—"

"Such things of power choose you, not you them. This has doubly come to you, from the hand of she who earned it and from your use of it. Take it up—its use may be over. But I think not."

Yonan had used sword and knife points to dig a pit, and he pushed the twisted, blackened rod into the earth. But as he did so he uttered an exclamation. For on the stone against which that thing had burnt there was now a boldly black picture— There grinned up at them a face which was more closely human than the one Kelsie had noted on the rod, yet so foully evil that she could not believe any such thing could exist. During its destruction it had painted its likeness on the stone, into the stone, for when Yonan strove to pick away at it with the point of his sword he could not scratch a single fragment of the sooty black free.

Dahaun strode around the rock and came back in a moment her hands cupped, holding water which dripped down from her curled fingers. She bent her head and breathed on what she held, reciting words—perhaps names. Then she turned to the witch who, plainly against her will, yet moved by a belief strong in her, dabbed one finger in the fast disappearing water and muttered some incantation of her own.

Next it went to Kemoc who passed his hand above the clasped ones of the Valley dweller and spoke his own prayer or ritual. Thereafter Dahaun went to the black mask on the stone and allowed the water to cascade down upon the burnt picture of the demonic head. Kelsie was sure she saw the lips of that writhe as if it would call out. But the image blurred, thinned, and was gone.

With her foot Dahaun prodded that stone into the hole after the remnants of the rod, then from her belt pouch took some withered leaves and allowed them to flutter down on top of that defiled bit of rock. Yonan struck with his sword. A cascade of gravel poured down, to utterly hide the buried. But it took them all—except the witch who made no move to help—to loosen and push over that burial of evil the stone with the carvings. Dahaun was the last to withdraw her hand, rather smoothing with her fingers those long eroded signs and symbols carven thereon.

"What manner of weapon was that?" Kemoc asked when they were done.

Dahaun shrugged. "Its like I have not seen. But in the days when this land was rent, adept fighting adept and no safety to be found save here in this Valley, there were many weapons which have been long forgotten. Who animated this— We have had a measure of uneasy peace since we fought the battle of the cliffs. I think that that is now at an end—or nearly so. The very fact that this could be planted above, perhaps to open a road to the Dark, is a threat I never thought we would see. The Sarn and the gray ones are up and out. If they stir so must the Thas and all the rest of the Dark. We must be ready to see perhaps something more than what lies here."

Kelsie held the bag with the Witch Jewel. She felt battered and bruised inside. There had been too much too soon. She knew that this was no dream. She had to believe Simon Tregarth, that by some chance she had come into an entirely new world where other natural laws held sway. Yet it was only with difficulty that she could make herself accept that. If she went back to the circle of the gate with the jewel she now held—if she passed between those standing stones—could she not win back to a life which was real—

Oh, this was real enough but it was not her reality. Simon

Tregarth seemed to have accepted it without question. But she—

"Keep you that—safe!" the harsh croak of the witch disturbed her thoughts then as the woman's angular form stepped close to Kelsie. One long pale finger stabbed the air in the direction of the packet she held.

"I am no witch," Kelsie returned, her dislike for the woman overriding all her caution at that moment.

The other laughed but there was only sneering amusement in that guttural sound. "Well may you say that, girl. But it seems that this Escore can turn upside down truths we know in Estcarp. Men hold power—" she favored both Yonan and Kemoc with a savage frown, "and those of no training wield the weapons of Light. But that has obeyed you once—"

"I gave no order!" Kelsie was quick to answer.

"If you did not—whence came the names you called upon? Out of the air which holds us all? What were you in your own time and place, girl? You have some power or that would not work for you. And an unknown power—" she shook her head, "who knows how it may hold when the times comes to face the Dark?"

Dahaun's hand fell again on Kelsie's arm, drawing her away from the witch toward the light trail descending into the heart of the Valley. "We have seen its work this day. I would say that you—and it—wrought mightily," she said to the girl. "Be not fearful—or only so much as to make you cautious. You bear now that which will be half protection, half weapon. Kaththea sent us word three tens of days ago that there was to come one who would be a balance for us in new struggles to come. It would seem that she was very right—"

"The babblings of a half witch—a traitor who fled from the place of learning before she was knit to the sisterhood," the witch was not to be overborne by Dahaun. Her sour mouth dropped the words like acid.

"She chose her own road," Dahaun said. "And now she

is Lady to Hilaron. Do you set even the combined forces of Estcarp against him, Wise Woman?"

"An adept? Who knows? In the old days it was those of his kind who rent the land."

"And in these days he helps to heal it!" countered Dahaun. "Enough, Wise Woman. You say you come to us for aid and yet you do nothing but question what is done. Perhaps Escore and Estcarp have grown too far apart in these days to be allies."

Her tone was very cool as she drew Kelsie with her, and they passed the witch on their way down into the Valley.

Six

Kelsie lay on the narrow sleeping mat. She had pushed aside the covering of net and feathers. Now she put one hand slowly, against her will, to underneath the higher end of the mat which served as a pillow.

Yes, it was still there—the wad of bag which held the Witch Jewel. She had tried to give it to Dahaun and now she remembered what had happened then with a shiver which did not spring from the night air about her.

It had moved—like some sluggish turtle or other living creature—the bag and its contents had moved—not through any doing of her own nor, she felt sure, through the action of Dahaun. Returning to lie again within close touch of her own hand. Willing or not it had been made plain that it meant to stay with her. Though how could one accord conscious feelings to a piece of crystal, no matter how finely wrought?

She rubbed her aching head. The pain which had come from the blow she had suffered when she fell through the "gate" had vanished at least two days ago. This was something which had come into being since she had taken up the crystal. It was as if within her head something stirred, struck against walls, bulging out to occupy more and more space.

Without truly knowing why she did so, Kelsie raised one hand, and, with outstretched forefinger, she drew a sign in the dark as one might paint upon a stretch of canvas. And—

The stone flared into life—showing through the cloth blue and bright for just an instant. How and why—those had begun to mean more now than "where" in the great hoard of questions which she wanted to have answered. Only those she had already asked had either received a flat denial of information or, as she suspected, a devious sidestepping from a clear reply.

"Who am—No, I am Kelsie McBlair!" she whispered aloud. Once more her thought followed that firmly beaten path. She had reached forward to stop McAdams' shot. He had struck her, sending her sprawling forward, and she had awakened in the circle of stones with the wildcat. Did the cat feel as strange as she? Or had Swiftfoot, now with her expected family, adjusted to this new territory without those raking questions which gave the girl so many sleepless hours in the night?

Gates—there were portals here and there in this ensorceled country which opened or shut, through which might come by design or chance castaways such as herself. Tregarth had told her there was no return. She forced herself to lie flat again, and, with her eyes squinted shut, she attempted by force of will to be again within the safe and well-known past.

Only that was difficult also. Why—Kelsie sat bolt upright again once more shivering.

Where had she been for those sharp instants out of time? Not back in the Scottish highlands. No! There had been a hall with many seats and at one end four chairs with tall backs and thronelike appearance set up on a dais before her. Not all the seats in that hall had been occupied—only two of the dais thrones. There had been a stirring about her—a feeling of expectancy and of the need for action—hurried action.

She rubbed her eyes with both hands as if she could reach through them into her head and so rub out that scene and the feeling it left in her, as if she were only a part of a great whole—that there was a need to be—what?

Now she reached beneath the pillow mat to seize the wrapped jewel and heave it away from her, as far away as she could send it. She went on her knees to the curtains which enforced the privacy of this sleeping quarter and drawing those aside she hurled the witch thing out and away. Then with a sigh of relief she settled back to sleep—or else to think her way out of this land and all the pitfalls it held for the stranger.

She twisted and turned, trying to hold in mind McAdams' angry face, the toppled stones behind him. That was what was true—the rest—

But it was the hall which closed about her. She was sitting in her proper seat, the one which had been assigned to her upon her taking the jewel oath, which would be hers through many, many years to come. To her left was an empty place—to her right, she was sure she heard the fluttering come and go of breath from Sister Wodelily. She could even smell clearly the scent of that flower which seemed to cling to the old woman's robes—it drowned out the spicy scent of the incense burning in braziers at either end of the dais.

They were supposed to be in meditation but her own thoughts skittered about. There was the lamb which had been found this morning beside its dead dam and which had been given to her to raise, there were the three gazia orphans she had found just a little while ago—surely the Second Lady would let her bring them into her own workroom to cherish. Were they not all oathbound to save life no matter how lowly on the scale? There was also the brewing of the tisane which so helped the pain of lower limbs in winter that they even bespoke commendation for her in the general assembly. She herself, Sister Makeease——Roylane——No! Never that name, even in her straying thoughts she must bury it so deeply that it could never be said again.

All thought of lambs, of herbs, or the quiet and gentle life she loved were driven from her by the words of the woman in the middle seat of the dais.

"Let the lots be drawn then."

A little before her was a wide-topped jar of time-aged silver and to this she was pointing with a rod which had appeared from the folds of her wide-skirted robe.

Within the bowl there was a fluttering, a rise of small bits of white as if someone had dumped there scraps of paper. They arose, their swirl forming a cloud as high as the head of the seated woman who had so commanded them, and now they traveled, swifter than any cloud, from above the dais out over the seats, those which were empty, alas, and those which still had occupants. Over each of the latter they made a quick revolution and they journeyed on. Then—one bit fell from that swarming cloud, fluttered down into the lap of a woman who sat five rows away from Sister Makeease. It was the dour-faced Sister Wittle that it so chose.

Sister Wittle! She wondered at the decision of the choice. Surely that was not influenced in any way. She had seen it in operation too many times and often enough it had fallen on some one of the sisterhood who seemed the least likely to be the proper one to handle the problem involved and still the end result had been success. Yet Sister Wittle to be sent as an emissary of the depleted Council—that was one of the oddest chances she had seen in many a year.

The cloud having loosed its first surprising choice was flitting on. Over one row it sped and then another. Now it was coming toward her. There was a sudden small cold feeling within her breast—the cloud was fast nearing the last of the number of the sisterhood who were eligible for any choice.

Above her head at last—and that white mote shifting down to lie upon her tightly clasped hands. No! But there

was no appeal. She must leave the warmth, the sisterhood—
she must travel out into the world which she had left what
now seemed so long ago. It was a wild land as yet bearing
the scars of war, one in which the sisterhood was not still
held in esteem. But there was no questioning the choice of
the lots—the bit of white rested on her like a burden which
grew heavier by the moment and from which there was no
escape.

She arose and the bit of white melted from her as might a
flake of snow. Sister Wittle was standing also and together
they moved forward to the foot of the dais looking up into
the face of All Mother, her features set in the mask of
perfect composure with which she faced each and every
change in the quiet passing of their days here.

"The lots have been cast and have chosen," she said in a
neutral voice. For a moment of forbidden questioning
Makeease wondered if All Mother was not as surprised at
those two choices as the rest—or most—had been. "The
Lord Warden has promised an escort through the mountains. The third day by the scry-cup is the most fortunate
one. You will find that which our far mothers knew, and
draw from it what we must have."

No question that they might fail in their task, she was as
firm with her words as if she had been sending them to the
storehouse to draw everyday supplies. But Makeease
wanted to cry out that she was no rightful one for this
sending—that she was weak in power and what she had was
for the easing of hurts not for the taking of something which
might be well guarded—by what she could not begin to
guess. Only here in the Refuge itself there had been tales in
plenty of things now wandering over mountain to plague the
land. They must go by their vows into the very heart of the
black unknown and take there what no one would rightfully
and freely give—the very strength of power!

"It is done," Sister Wittle spoke aloud but Sister
Makeease could not even shape the words with her stiff lips.

No—

Kelsie was sitting up once more on her sleeping mat. She was *not* that one. Her outflung hand bore down to steady herself and there was something under it. She held so the very stone in its bag which she had hurled away earlier. But she was herself—not that other one—truly it was so. She shut her eyes and snatched her hand from its grip upon the shrouded jewel, concentrating upon her own memories. She had been working in the kennels with the puppy when the telegram had come.

Someone she had heard of only as a kind of tale—Old Jessie McBlair, the aunt of her long dead father, was gone— leaving her a house and what was left of a once large estate. She must claim it herself said the will the lawyer explained.

So she had gone to Scotland with high hopes of a home of her own at last—only to be faced by a ruin in which only one wing was barely habitable and that fast falling in upon itself into the bargain. There had been sullen and surly faces to front her and no liking for the place or the people had been born in her during the few days she had been there—before this had happened. She was no daughter of power—

She huddled together, her knees against her chest, her arms laced to hold them so. The hand which in her sleep had somehow summoned the jewel bag was tingling and she believed that she could see a faint bluish light about the pouch until she kicked an edge of the covering over it.

There was movement in the dusk of the small, curtain-walled cubicle and she smelled the musky scent of the wildcat. The yellow eyes viewed her from near floor level.

"Go home to your kittens!" Kelsie whispered. "Have you not made enough trouble for me when you brought that—that thing into the Valley?"

She did not expect any answer from the cat, certainly not this sudden thrust of compulsion—that she must be alert— that there was that which needed her attention. The girl fought it with all the willpower in her. Perhaps it was that other one she had seen in her dream—been in her dream—who took command now. For against her will Kelsie loosed that tight grip upon herself, took up the bag and put it into the front of her laced shirt where it lay warm and pulsating as if it held sentient life of its own. She had carried small animals so in past days and felt the same glow of life against her skin.

Still under the order she could not break, she arose and took up the hooded cloak they had given her, sat again to pull on the soft half boots, fastened tightly her belt. Swiftfoot was moving back and forth impatiently before her though she did not offer any cry. Now she stretched forth her blunt muzzle and caught, with sharp teeth, the corner of that cloak, giving a pull toward the direction of the door.

Kelsie obeyed—both that and the force which had settled on her own will muffling her fear and her stubborn need for freedom—moving silently into the night. There was a moon riding high but yet giving a full light to the small gathering of buildings. Still pulling at the cloak edge the cat steered her toward the cliffs. One foot before the other, fighting that drive all the way Kelsie covered much of the same way she had taken in the day.

Twice she passed sentries and both times it was as if they did not see her. There was no challenge, no notice of her going and her own voice would not answer her command to call out. Fear grew in her, blotting out a little of the order which had set her moving. She strove to turn but there was no such thing possible.

Already they had reached the rock which by Dahaun's order had been moved to stand upon the place where the artifact of evil had been buried. There the cat paused and dropped its hold upon her cloak edge, snarled and pawed at a small stone sending it whirling against the large rock. But it was not to view this battlefield of sorts that Kelsie had been moved here. For the cat was going on, climbing another rock. And where Swiftfoot went Kelsie seemed bound to follow.

There was a narrow break in the wall of the heights and from it came a mewling sound. Swiftfoot sprang forward and the girl stumbled after. She had to duck to avoid the heavy rock overhead. There was a narrow passage and then, dark as it was, she felt space about her. From somewhere came a wind carrying with it a foul odor. She heard the cat snarl and then the sound of a struggle and she wavered back against the wall too blinded by the darkness to try to reach the scene of battle.

A body thrust against her in that dark and her skin was rasped by coarse hair or fur while something caught at her hand and tried to jerk her toward the sounds of the struggle. She used her other hand to catch at the bag and pull out of it the Witch Jewel.

The burst of light was eye dazzling to her but apparently painfully blinding to the thing which had attacked her. She saw a mound of what looked like tangled roots flatten itself as far as it could to the ground. While the wave of light swept on to encounter and hold another dire sight, Swiftfoot before the three kittens, the cubling being at least half her size, facing with bared teeth and claws two more of the evil smelling creatures of the dark.

Thas! Though Kelsie could not remember having more than heard the name in passing, now her mind instantly identified these lurkers in the dark. She swung out the jewel by its chain and there were guttural cries from the trio in the cave. The one at her feet was crawling as might a giant insect after the other two, still standing backed away, their crooked fingered hands over the matted stuff covering the upper parts of their faces, hiding their eyes.

Back they edged and now Kelsie came away from the wall against which she had taken shelter and continued to swing out the jewel its light growing ever brighter. She was aware of a draining down her arm, through her fingers and into the chain, as if she herself was the energy which had revitalized the thing and brought about this awakening.

The attackers fled while Swiftfoot licked her litter, still

raising her head to snarl now and again. What the trio sought was a tumble of earth and stone at the back of this slitlike cave, apparently the burrow through which they had made entrance here. The first of them reached that and threw itself forward as one might enter surf pounding on the shore of a sea. There was a frenzied scrabbling and an upward shower of earth and small stones. Taking heart at the very visible fear of the noisome invaders Kelsie resolutely drove the other two after the first. She faced now a hole through which she would have to creep in order to advance and she had no intention of doing that. However, she continued to stand and wave the jewel back and forth until her arm tired and fell heavily by her side, as weary as if she had been carrying some great weight.

Nor was it only her arm which was limp with fatigue, her whole body was suddenly struck by a feeling of great lassitude so that she sank to her knees before that evil smelling opening, the light of the jewel fading to a dim glow.

Thas—the underground workers of evil. The very name in her mind appeared to open a door of knowledge. How dared they come into the Valley? There were age old guardians here and those the People of Green Peace believed could not be broached. Yet had the Thas not chanced into the cave Swiftfoot had chosen as her den what might they have done?

"Much!" That answer to her thought was spoken aloud and she nearly sprawled on her face as she strove to swing around to confront the speaker.

Wittle stood there. The gray of her robe faded into the shadow so only her bone-white face and her hands, cupping her own jewel where it swung about her throat, could be clearly seen. For the first time since she had first met her Kelsie saw no animosity in the witch's expression. Instead Wittle was studying Kelsie with an intensity which had something of astonishment in it.

"You are—" her voice was hardly above a whisper.

"Kelsie McBlair!" The girl flashed back. For all her dreaming this night she would hold to that with every bit of strength she could summon.

"She—she chose you then—it is the truth. She exercised the choice!"

"I am not Makeease—" Kelsie denied.

"You have that of her in you now whether you will it or not!"

Wittle's hands dropped away from cupping about her own jewel and it broke into a clear blue light. The stink of the Thas seemed to disappear and Kelsie's strength began to return so that she was able to stand without feeling that her legs were ready to give way under her.

"This must be closed," Wittle was past her in two strides to face the hole. Swinging her jewel by its chain, even as Kelsie had earlier swung the one she carried, she began to recite a cadence of words, words which called upon the very earth itself to provide a stopper to evil. The air between her jewel and the opened earth was filled with ever changing symbols which curled in and out and at times seemed to catch upon one another and cling. Until there was formed a kind of net which floated on until it crashed between the pile of excavated earth and the wall behind it.

"Be it so!" The three words crackled like a flash of lightning across a storm rolled sky. Instantly stone and rock moved, were tossed, pounded, driven back into a firm wall once again. Still glowing therein were flecks of blue as if the net still held. The witch had already turned her back on what she had wrought and was again measuring Kelsie with narrow eyes.

"The Sisterhood grows smaller each year," she said, as if she were reminding herself of something. "Perhaps it is to the gates we must look—and Makeease at her dying saw the truth. You are of us whether you won your jewel by lessoning or by gift—"

"I am not!" Kelsie dared to deny that. Wittle had always been her enemy, why now was she changing, subtly calling upon Kelsie to join forces with her?

"I do—" Again it was as if the other read her thoughts. "We were sent and we have not yet obeyed that sending—"

"I am not a witch." Somewhat to the girl's surprise the witch inclined her head in answer to that.

"By our laws you are not. Yet Makeease knew it. Though perhaps it was because she was on the edge of death that it was made clear to her. You cannot deny what lies in you now—"

"There is nothing in me!"

Kelsie backed away, even as she had during the night dark attack of the Thas, until her shoulders were against the rough, cold stone. Perhaps she would have run— But she could not! That same compulsion which had brought her here had swooped back, to seize upon her once again. She could have screamed in her rage and fear. That she was not master of her own body was the most frightening thing of all. Yet she could not take the single step which would carry her past the witch and on her way out of here.

The girl said in a voice she fought to keep from trembling. "Stop playing your tricks on me and let me go."

Wittle swept both arms outward in a gesture which offered Kelsie full freedom. "I play no tricks. Look within yourself to see what lies there now."

Look inward? Kelsie tried, not sure of what the witch might mean. She discovered that, without knowing it, she had set the chain of the jewel about her own neck and it, pulsating, rested on her breast even as Wittle wore hers.

She gasped a ragged breath.

"What would you have me do?" she asked in a small voice. The drain she experienced was not yet repaired, she felt as if, should she stand away from the wall, she might fall.

"Breathe so—" Wittle was drawing deep, slow breaths. "Think of your body, of the feet, the legs which support you—of the blood which runs through them nourishing, cleansing. Your body has served you well, think kindly of it, slow—ah, slow, sister. Think of having slept through the night sweetly with no dreams to disturb your rest. It is morning and you awaken renewed, filled, mistress of yourself, sister to your jewel which will serve you now even if you try to send it away. Come—"

Without waiting to see if Kelsie obeyed her or not, Wittle bent her tall form and left the cave and indeed the girl discovered that she was drawn after. There was still silver moonlight among the rocks and the witch sought out a place where the beams were full. She stood there, her arms upraised and out, as if she desired to indeed draw the moon down into her hold. Hesitatingly Kelsie followed suit.

Her jewel was glowing again. Not with the forceful blue it had shone when it had stood against the Thas, but with a pure white light. It warmed and the warmth spread through her also, so that the last of that backaching fatigue was banished. She felt rather as if indeed she had awakened into a good day and had bathed cleanly at the pool in the Valley, that all was well within her and that she had already accomplished much that she had been set to do.

How long they stood there Kelsie could not reckon, but at length Wittle lowered her arms as a shadow of stone crept to them and there appeared a cloud touching the moon shield overhead.

"Good—" Her voice held a sigh. "So it is with the power when one uses it. It draws, ah, how it can draw," there was remembered pain in her voice then, "but there is always the renewing. How is it with you now, Makeease—" then she hesitated, "No, for one there is one name, for another another. You have received no name in company—"

"I am Kelsie!" Some of her old antagonism flared.

"Do you not understand," she had never expected Wittle to show such patience, "to use your birthing name so boldly is to invite the ill to enter. It will offer a key to that which we must fear the more. The body can be ill used by the Dark Ones, yes. But it is the worse when the inner part is touched. Perhaps it is different with you and the naming of names is not a danger."

"Sometimes perhaps," Kelsie had a sudden memory of times which a name might bring a person into danger even in her own time and place—perhaps not the same kind of danger, but peril as her world knew it. "Yet we do not change them—" No, that was not so either. People did change their names, their very kinds of life—what of witnesses and spies? Still she was neither and her name was a part of herself she was not prepared to surrender, for by doing so she might well join herself even tighter to wild adventure.

Seven

The witch reached behind one of the rocks and drew forth a backpack, and then another which she slung over to fall at Kelsie's feet. The girl edged back and away from it.

"What are you doing?" she demanded.

"We go," Wittle returned calmly. "What we were sent to do lies still before us. If we wait upon the favor of these of the Valley we may never reach it. They war when attacked or when the Shadow draws too near, they do not invade its own places."

"I won't!" Kelsie watched Wittle draw her arms through the lashings of her own pack, settling it on her shoulders with a shrug.

"You cannot now do otherwise. You have used the jewel—it is yours and you are its."

Kelsie would have fled away from this mad woman, taken the trail down back to the Valley. But once more her body rebelled against her will. With warmth from the stone flooding through her, she discovered she must also stoop, pick up that burden and prepare to carry it.

"Do not fight it, girl," the witch's voice held its old superior and contemptuous ring. "You are of the sisterhood whether or no and this is the geas laid upon you."

Thus against all her desires she began to climb, following Wittle farther and farther up the steep slopes using toes and fingers, striving to compensate for the backward pull of her burden. They reached the top of that barrier which nature, or those who dealt so close to nature that they could summon her services on demand, had set about the Valley. Beyond was a country which seemed to draw more shadow than light from the moon, to be truly a place of peril. That Wittle was calmly descending into that, taking Kelsie with her, the girl could not retreat.

If there were sentries and watchers on duty in those heights (Kelsie was sure that there were) the witch had her own method of passing unseen and was able also to encompass Kelsie. For there arose no one to bid them halt or inquire what they would do.

There was a usable trail which zigzagged down the opposite side of the heights and they did not take it swiftly, Wittle making methodically sure of her footing while Kelsie followed close behind her.

Once a winged blot of darkness flew swiftly over them and the witch stood still, Kelsie freezing into a similar halt. But the thing did not return, and, after a time in which Kelsie drew short shallow breaths, Wittle once more started on. Again she froze into immobility, startling Kelsie so that she nearly ran into the pack the other wore when there sounded a single ear-grating howl from the lowlands toward which they were going. This time Wittle hissed an order to the girl:

"A gray one. Put your jewel into hiding! They have eyes which can comb the darkest shadow." She was fumbling with her own jewel, holding open the neck opening of her own robe and dropping her glowing gem within the inner folds. Kelsie followed and nearly yelped aloud. For the heat that the stone now emitted was such as if she had slipped a live coal against the skin of her breast.

Wittle appeared to believe that this was the only precaution they need take, for she was striding on again. Kelsie, perforce, still drawn by that overriding other will, must follow.

They came to the stream which burrowed a way through

the mountains to feed the Valley river and here the witch kilted up her long robe so that her thin white legs were bare to her knees, motioning for Kelsie to shuck her soft boots even as the witch abandoned her sandals.

Free of foot Wittle stepped into the shallows of the stream and marched confidently forward Kelsie again behind. Perhaps it was because she had a need for establishing her superiority again that the witch whispered:

"Running water is disaster to some of the Dark Ones. It is best to hold to it while one can."

Trying to keep her own voice low Kelsie demanded with what small power she could summon:

"Where are we going?" That she was following one she did not trust was the stark truth, but if she could summon the strength of the jewel again perhaps she could break free of Wittle should the other release any of the control she had established. Meanwhile to humor her might be best.

"Where we are led," was the very unsatisfactory answer she was given. "As you know—no," the witch corrected herself. "You who are one of us and yet not one—perhaps the knowing was not given with the jewel. We seek the source of the ancient power—that which formed our sisterhood in the beginning and where we must stand again to gather to us that which will raise up anew all that we were once. That it lies to the east is all that we know. Sister Makeease was questing for it—"

"And she died!" The cold of her own frightened self fought the warmth of the jewel she wore. "What promise have you that your purpose can be served—"

"She went with guards—she rode openly though the warning was clear. But she would not listen to those of the Valley," Wittle's tone was once more cold and sharp. "This is not a search which can be done by a trampling force of clumsy men. She was wrong and so she paid for it. We shall search by night and this—" she cupped her hand over the wan glow shining through her robe, "shall be our guide. For we brought the jewels out of this land in the ancient days and they will be drawn to that which gave them their first life. This much we can be sure of. If we watch them carefully by their waxing and their waning shall we be guided."

"What if," Kelsie moistened her lower lip with her tongue tip before she continued, "this source you seek is now held by the Dark?"

"It may be besieged by the Dark well enough," Wittle agreed, "but taken it has not been or our stones would die. The Light and the Dark cannot lie together."

"Shadows and moonlight do," Kelsie was finding apter words of protest than she had known existed in her mind.

"The Moon is at full, as long as it remains so we can draw sustenance from it. When it begins to wane," the witch hesitated, "then we tread even more carefully."

It was clear that she had a vast confidence in herself and Kelsie, as wary as she was, was cowed by that as they went forward through the night, keeping to the stream as their roadway. When the first shafts of gray dawn appeared along the horizon the witch pointed ahead to where a sandbar projected well into the stream. On three sides it was surrounded by water, which flowed with a swifter current in midstream. The fourth was connected to the land by a narrow neck on which drift had caught in a tangle as if there had been some recent storm which had brought such debris out of the land before them.

The witch waded out on this neck of land and Kelsie gratefully followed, though she had to tread over gravel as well as the sand. Then they were ashore and Wittle shed her pack, Kelsie following her example, her shoulders aching from the strain put upon them. But if she were tired from their night's tramp, Wittle was not. Already the witch had approached the drift and was pulling at pieces of it, working crooked branches around to form a barrier across the narrow scrap of land which connected them with the shore. She was plainly building a barricade, though what such a defense might save them from Kelsie had no idea. That Wittle appeared to think this important set her working beside the witch.

It was not until they had a breast-high barrier there that Wittle seemed satisfied and went back to her pack, worrying open the strap around its midsection to bring out a packet of wilted leaves fast lashed about. She freed those also and Kelsie saw that she had a flat cake of some darkish substance from which she broke a small piece and began to nibble around its edge.

"Eat," she sputtered through a full mouth and gestured toward Kelsie's own discarded pack. The girl found a leaf-wrapped parcel within containing the same rations, and tasted a bite gingerly. Though its looks were not encouraging the flavor was better and she got it down, washed by several palmfuls of water from the stream.

However, here on this patch of sand, though barricaded as it now was from the land, she had no sense of security. Thus as she watched Wittle settle herself on her bundle for sleep in the early morning Kelsie wondered at the unconcern of the witch. Was she so very sure that they were in complete safety?

"Trust your jewel, girl—" Wittle's eyes were closed but it was as if that allowed her to discern Kelsie's thoughts better. "The Dark hunts mainly by night—"

"Then why do we—?" began Kelsie bewildered.

"Travel by dark?" Wittle finished for her. "Because as long as the full moon is overhead we can cast for the better that trail we must discover. Where the Dark masses—there we may discover the seed we seek."

Wittle might be very sure of herself and her methods of hunting but Kelsie did not agree. The witch was breathing evenly asleep while the girl still sat looking around her with a wariness which was an ever present part of her now.

The stream ran across the plain until it reached the hills over which they had come during the night. She could sight some moving humps in the distance ahead to the east which she thought might be animals browsing. The sky was very clear, with not even a trace of cloud, and once in a while again to the east some shape flapped lazily across it.

There was life in the stream also. Now and then a fish

broke the surface of the water chasing one of the gauzy winged insects which near filled the air only a few inches above the river, engaged in some complicated dance or maneuvers of their own. Then there crawled out in the sandbank a lizardlike creature as long as her forearm which paid no attention to the two already occupying that stretch of territory but wheeled about its head pointing waterwards and apparently went to sleep in the rapidly warming sun.

Though the plain stretched well to the east there were also the irregular lines of hills or mountains to be sighted beyond and here and there were dark clumps of trees gathered in thick copses as if they had been deliberately planted so. There were also tumbles of stone perhaps a half mile farther on which to Kelsie suggested ruins of a very ancient and now unidentifiable building. While the tall grass of the meadowland, already beginning to brown under the sun's searing heat, was troubled now and again, not by any wind (for the dawn breeze had died away and there was no movement of air at all). Those waving fronds and blades must mark the comings and goings of small life.

The sun was hot and she found her head nodding, her eyes shutting of themselves. At length she chose a place closer to the barrier they had woven from the drift and, in spite of her wariness, fell asleep.

What nightmare awoke her, shaking and sweating, she could not piece together once her eyes were fully open. Perhaps it was just as well that her waking mind repudiated that memory for the fear carried over and she huddled shivering by the mass of drift.

Wittle lay exactly as she had when Kelsie had gone to sleep. Almost she could believe that the witch had died save that her breast rose and fell with long deep breaths. The creature from the stream was gone again and—

Kelsie looked about her for a weapon. There was a water smoothed root bigger at one end than the other. She worried that loose, winning so a crude club. She must have slept half the day or more away—the sun was to the westward. But though the land looked as peaceful as it had before, she was sharply aware that there was something moving toward them through the tall grass.

Very slowly she pivoted where she still knelt, giving each section she could see a questioning survey. Those moving stands of grass which she had earlier believed marked the coming and going of the inhabitants of this land were no longer in evidence. There was a stillness over the whole of the land which instinct told her was not natural. Then she heard the splash of water and turned instantly to front the screen of willows downstream.

A figure pushed through them, treading as she and Wittle had done barefooted in the water, his boots slung by their lacing cords about his neck. He was fully armed and the metallic links of light mail which formed a veiling about the helm he wore showed only a very small portion of his face. Yet she knew him.

"Yonan," her word was but a whisper but it appeared to carry to him for he threw up one hand, whether in salute or warning she did not know—in this time and place she took it for the latter.

She was on her feet, though she still grasped the club, and her own wave was a vigorous one, beckoning him on. Had he been sent to take them back? She would indeed welcome such a summons, if this strange compulsion she was caught up in would allow her.

As she and Wittle he wore a small backpack, and, seeing that, she was not so sure that his coming meant the end of their journeying. There was an angry exclamation from behind her as Wittle moved forward, to stand nearly at the water's edge watching that newcomer.

"What do you here?" demanded the witch while he was still some distance from them, her voice low but carrying over the splashing he made as he moved.

"What I am sent to do," he returned. One of the veil strips of his helm swung free, and Kelsie could see by the set of his firm chin a suggestion that he was angered.

"We do not need you—" Wittle's voice was that of Swiftfoot's hissing growl.

"Perhaps that is so," he replied, now near enough to wade out of the stream, by his very coming forcing the witch back a step or two. "This is a troubled land, we will not have it troubled further— Return to the Valley lest you be taken. There are mighty forces on the move."

"Who has been a-scrying and read that in her bowl?" Wittle's contempt once more ruled her voice. "Certainly this is a troubled land. Perhaps we move to put an end to some of that troubling. Let us reach the force and—"

"And be blasted by your own folly? Well enough, if that means that only you will suffer. But each bit of the power is precious and to risk it in the midst of enemies—"

Kelsie saw Wittle's hands snap upward to jerk at the jewel chain and bring her gem out of hiding. Even in the daylight its blue fire was not diminished. She took it in one hand and pointed it toward Yonan.

He laughed and swung his sword out of its sheath, holding the blade and raising the blue stone grip between them. There was a flash from the jewel, a similar answer from the stone, and those two met, pushing each other until there was nothing left but a wisp of smoke.

"You—you—" for the first time Kelsie saw Wittle truly at a loss for words, her usual arrogance gone.

"Yes, I am not for your guiding, Lady Witch," he said. "We have discovered other bits of power ourselves. Quan iron, in the hand of he who dares to carry it, lives. Now that we have settled that you are not to be so easily rid of me," he allowed his pack to fall from his shoulders, "let us discuss the matter. The Lady Dahaun has sent a message to Hilaron. Do you also think that you have the power to stand against an adept? He feels strongly about this land and will not allow tricks to be played which will bring in the shadow forces past our control."

"What would you do?" Wittle asked sullenly.

"Go with you. Do you not realize that we are as eager to mark sources of power as you are? That we must know what lies hidden whenever we can that the Dark does not reach it first?"

"This is no affair for men—"

"This is an affair for any who dare it!" he countered. "As a scout, and one who has dared before, it is my choice to come on this quest. You head for the Sleepers—"

Wittle's head jerked as if he had struck her across the mouth. "How know you that?" she demanded and for once there was flaming heat instead of the cold in her voice.

Yonan shrugged. "Think you that you can keep such purpose hidden in the Valley? We have known all the time you waited for your sister what it was that you would do."

She glared at him and her hand tightened on her jewel as if she would again strive to try strength against strength with him. But he had already turned to Kelsie.

"You do this of your free will?" he asked.

"No, but not because of her urging," she replied. "There is something in the jewel which has claimed me."

"Take it off!" That was more an order than a request and her hands moved to obey—moved only a fraction. The stone blazed hot beneath her jerkin as if in warning.

"I can't," she was forced to admit.

What she could see of his face was a frown. "Touch—" He held forth his sword by the blade and the blue band in the hilt had a subdued fire of its own. Kelsie reached for the hilt and then dropped her hand with a small cry of surprise. Her fingers were numb and that deadness was creeping across her palm and up her arm. "I can't—"

He nodded as if he had expected that very answer from her. "You are under a geas."

"A what?"

"An order from some Old One or adept. Perhaps it lies in the heart of that stone you wear. That you must obey now that it is set upon you."

Wittle laughed unpleasantly. "Think you that you can wear a stone of power and escape the payment it calls from its wearer? You are set upon this path now whether you will or not."

It seemed to Kelsie then that this whole venture had been imposed on her even before the jewel of the dying witch had come into her life.

"I'm not one of you," she protested. "Why must I be

drawn into this?'' It was a question that she might have asked hours earlier but it was not until the coming of Yonan that some bit of reality had broken into that drive which had held her.

"You have no choice," Wittle turned and walked a step or so away to settle once more on the sand, her back to them, plainly preparing to return to the sleep from which Yonan had awakened her. Kelsie looked to the young man.

"I do not choose—" she began when he shook his head.

"Lady, in this land our choices are limited. I, myself, have walked strange ways because I was caught up in something which was stronger than any will of mine. This is a haunted place and what haunts it are bits and pieces of old struggles and old commands, which, once voiced, still hold. We have held against the Dark for many seasons now but there have always been rumors that inland," he pointed with his chin upriver as he still held his sword in his two hands, "there are pockets of ancient power which are neither allied with the Dark nor with the Light. If such can be found, and what you wear is indeed a key to it or them, then there is purpose in what we do here."

"Purpose but not choice!" she said bitterly. Her failure to touch the sword had given her a shock which had somehow awakened her out of the bemused state which she now recognized must have encompassed her since they left the Valley.

"Purpose but no choice," he agreed quietly. "Now, will you rest, Lady, this is the last night of the full moon and after that we shall move by day. And how far we travel, who can tell?"

Feeling was returning to her hand as she rubbed it vigorously. She wanted to argue but his complete acceptance of what seemed to have happened to her made her believe there would be no profit in that. She sought out her own bed in the sand and pillowing her head on her pack allowed herself to relax. She had not really expected sleep but it came and quickly.

She roused when an ungentle hand was laid on her

shoulder and it was to look up into a sky with scudding clouds and the first drops of rain coming with the evening. Wittle stood over her, pack already on her shoulders, a piece of the dried journey cake in her hand.

"Time to go—" the witch said after she swallowed. Her shoes were once more in her belt and she waved toward the water. Yonan stood on the edge of the stream itself, the water curling up as far as his knees.

"We cannot take to this too long," he commented as Kelsie found her own provisions and chewed at the dry bits which rasped her tongue and gums. "There may have been a hard rain upstream—the water is rising."

But they did begin the night's trek splashing through the water. While the few drops which had fallen became part of a downpour to soak through Kelsie's clothing and set her shivering—though neither of her companions seemed to take any notice of the storm.

The night came fast though the clouds were illuminated now and then by flashes of lightning and there was the drumbeat of thunder to follow. The waves of the stream washed Kelsie up to mid-thigh now and she could feel the pull of the current. Once her foot connected painfully with a rock and she might have fallen had not Yonan's hand caught and held her up.

At length they were driven to the shore and huddled under the wide spreading branches of a willow to put on their foot gear. In the dark of the night and the storm her two companions were only half-seen blots and she wondered how they could keep together and whether it might not do well to stay in the flimsy shelter they had found until the storm passed.

She felt Yonan stir first and then came his low-pitched voice through the clamor of the rain and the stream.

"Do you smell it?"

She obediently sniffed, but all she was aware of was a musty, earthy scent which she vaguely associated with the wet ground. Yonan got to his feet and started away from the water. By the lightning flash she saw the gleam of his sword, drawn and ready in his hand. At the same time the flesh of her upper arm was bruised by a harsh grip of the witch seeming intent on holding her where she was.

There was a sound like a shout cut in half and Yonan disappeared into the ground. Kelsie broke away from the witch and ran forward only to have her feet swept from under her and feel herself falling. She thought she screamed and the jewel at her breast burst into a strong light as she landed, knocking Yonan face down into wet earth which was all about them. There was truly a stench here, one she had smelled before.

Thas! They had fallen into one of the underground ways of those dark dwellers. Wittle made no such mistake as Kelsie's and she did not join them in their tangle of arms and legs. By the time they had regained their feet in the hole one whole side of mudlike, noisome sledge fell in upon them, sending them to their knees again and nearly burying them.

Kelsie strove to escape when, out of the deeper dark which marked that part of the tunnel which had survived the cave-in there snaked a thick length of what seemed a root and it settled about her drawing tight enough to make her gasp as it pinned her arms to her body.

Eight

Another coarse-skinned line struck about her hips and in a moment all her struggling could not move her, except as her bonds wished, and she was being drawn straight to the shadowed side of the pit where there was an opening. By the floundering noises which she heard, Yonan was faring little, if any, better.

On her breast the jewel glowed, and she caught a faint glimmer ahead which might mark the power inset on Yonan's sword hilt. By the light she herself carried she could see now that what held her in bondage looked to be two thick roots. Yet they had the mobility of serpents and by these she was being pulled roughly along, bumped from wall to wall, down a passage intended for creatures smaller than herself. Dank earth smeared her all over and she was spitting to clear it from her mouth.

Also the scent which thickened the air was stomach churning and Kelsie had to battle the nausea which arose to choke her throat. She judged from sounds that Yonan was being forced along behind her as she heard exclamations of disgust and anger.

It seemed to her that that passage lasted at least an hour or more—though it could not have in truth. Then she was jerked like a cork out of a bottle into a place where there was a ghastly phosphorescent light, such as might come from something rotten, proceeding from the tops of crooked stakes set up in a square. Into this trap the ropes snapped her and a moment later she was bowled over by Yonan landing hard against her as her bonds withdrew and his followed.

There was a crunching sound. A rock taller and wider than her own body had fallen to close the gap in the cold fire of the palings around them. Yonan was already on his feet and facing that doorway.

The tops of the palings, where that weird light gleamed, were well above her head as she got to her feet. There the light gathered into an unwholesome mist which hid from sight what might lie directly over them. She crossed her arms, rubbing the bruises near her shoulders where the ropes had cut the hardest. There seemed to be scratches there which smarted under her touch as if the rough surface of the rope had rubbed the skin bare. Yonan, because of his mail, must have fared much better.

He had given but a short inspection to the stone which served as a door and was now prowling along the side of the square, sword out and ready as if he expected some instant move against them. At length he aimed at a crack between two of the palings and levered but the steel made no impression on the giant fence.

"Your jewel," he said abruptly, "can it cut our way clear?"

The gem still blazed, but it seemed to Kelsie that the light was less, as if the waning beams from the paling smothered it. However, obediently she stepped closer to the nearest fetid smelling pillar and held up the stone so that a lesser beam of the blue light focused directly.

To her eyes the wood, root, or stone, whatever that fencing might be, did writhe under the prod of the light. However, when Yonan, with an exclamation, pushed beside her to add his sword tip to the spot of light there was nothing but an adamant surface there.

"Where are we?" Kelsie tried to tamp down her rising fear by asking in the most normal voice she could produce.

He shrugged. "In Thas hands. Where? We can be anywhere, as far as the outer world is concerned."

"Wittle—"

"I do not think she was caught."

"These Thas—"

"Serve the Dark," he interrupted. "They hunt in packs and so can better pull us down. And their root ropes are harsh holding."

"What do they want?"

"Beyond just evil mischief? I would say that jewel of yours. Probably not for themselves, they are servants of more mighty masters and have probably gone to report to those now. Soon we shall see what manner of the Dark they serve."

"My jewel—" She slipped the chain over her head, allowing it now to dangle from her fingers and began to swing it back and forth. In her mind she concentrated upon it, bedazzled by the pulsation of its light as if she had never seen it so before. That waxing and waning followed a beat which began slowly but arose to draw faster and faster flashes from the stone.

Her own heart was beating quickly, in time with the stone? Of that she could not be sure. Nor did it matter. What did was that she must hold the jewel in her sight, concentrate on it completely, forgetting all else.

It was difficult at first, that concentration. Then in the whirl of light which followed the path of the jewel she saw something begin to form. There was no mistaking those hard features. Wittle! Yet the witch was not there, only a small semblance of her. Still Kelsie focused her full attention on that face and it seemed to her that Wittle was staring back as if she, too, could see them.

"Out!" Kelsie spoke the one word which meant the most to her now.

She watched Wittle's mouth open. If the witch spoke the

girl did not hear her with her ears. However, into her mind flashed what might be an answer or even some mischief of the enemies. She stopped the whirl of the jewel with her other hand. The face of Wittle abruptly vanished.

But now she held the stone on her palm in spite of the heat it generated, which seemed enough to sear her flesh from her bones. Yet still she held and pointed a single shaft of light, governed by her tormented fingers, not at the stake before her where Yonan had made his attack but rather to its crown where the yellowish evil-smelling haze arose from some unsighted fire.

The point of that light thrust struck the haze, cut through it. She saw a bowl on the top of the shaft. It was that the light was attacking. She watched a blue spot appear on that side, grow not only in size but in brilliance. Then something dropped at their feet and the bowl showed a wide section shorn from it. Into that opening Kelsie beamed her light. But it was not enough. Into her mind spun that knowledge. She had not the full power she should have been able to summon—as a witch she was flawed by knowing far too little.

She spoke without turning her head. "Give to me the Quan iron. Lay it upon my wrist."

Kelsie might have asked him to supply a brand to burn her past all healing. She gnawed at her lower lip, determined not to cry out—to forget the pain of her body, to concentrate only on what she had done and would do.

For that strip of blue metal was like a second force, feeding into the hands she had cupped about the jewel. The raw pain of it she would have to bear but the pulsations of the light grew greater and closer together, firing up the jewel's azure beam.

Then—

There was a roar—had she heard that with her ears or sensed the final confrontation of force against force in her body? From the now shattered bowl at the top of the stake shot another flash of light momentarily as vivid as lightning across the sky so far above them now. The haze itself appeared to catch from that flame and billow out not yellow now, nor blue but forming a white glare which punished her eyes until she had to close them. Something struck her shoulder, another object grazed her hip. She heard Yonan cry out. A mailed arm closed about her waist in an ungentle grasp dragging her back against his body as he, too, retreated. Her arms wavered and fell though she did not drop the stone except to spin by the chain she still held.

Above their heads there wove back and forth ribbons of fire and these coiled about the stakes which made up the walls of their cage. They burned then, those stakes, crackling open as might flesh caught in a blast of flame. The heat ate in as the two now crouched in the midst of the circle. Above the crackling of that fire Kelsie was sure she heard voices shouting a guttural refrain, but she could see nothing now for she had shielded her eyes from that searing display with one forearm. She was not even aware whether the stone had finished its mad spinning or not.

The crackling and the stench became worse. She was gasping and felt the similar labor of Yonan's chest against her as they fought for breath amid the conflagration.

As yet the burning debris had fallen outward, she guessed, for the heat which struck at them was airborne, not from the gutted remnants of the stakes. Slowly that heat declined. At last Kelsie felt able to uncover her eyes and look about her. There were stubs of the stakes still showing ribs of spark producing fire. But outside that destruction there writhed and flailed those captor roots which had dragged them here. Now and then when one of the butt stumps blazed up the girl was certain she caught sight of some scurrying creature which in this light looked like a wadded pack of rootlets. It was possible that the owners of this trap were spinning another now, a more substantial cage for their captives.

Yonan moved from beside her, slowly, as if worn-out

after a long day of tramping. While she was too tired to move at all. He tottered toward the nearest hole in the wall where the paling had burnt clear down to its root in the stone and with his sword he cut and stabbed at the small core of flame-eaten wood still showing above the surface. Then he held out his hand to her.

"Come!"

"Can't you see that is just what they want us to do—they are waiting there," she answered. She greatly doubted at that moment she could do no more than crawl on her hands and knees, and so provide easy meat for those waiting beyond.

He came back to her in two quick strides, and, his hand under her armpit, pulled her up to her feet.

"They are confused," he said as he half led, half supported her to the exit he had contrived. "Whatever lord they serve—neither he nor his higher servants can be here now."

Kelsie could not see how he was so sure of that. But she was too tired to argue and she needed what strength and courage she had left not to waste in futile argument, but to be ready to face what lay beyond. That the breaking of the cage set them entirely free she doubted very much indeed.

They stepped over the narrow path fire that Yonan's sword had opened for them. In the failing light from the almost destroyed paling she could see that indeed roots crawled across the floor, the nearer ones heading for them.

Yonan made a quick thrust to his left, not using the point of his sword but bringing down the hilt sharply against the raised end of the nearest root length. The thing squirmed and drew back. On its surface where the iron must have touched there was an oval of light which spread swiftly as if power continued to eat into it.

It was then that Kelsie heard clearly a dull thud, a thud which was drumlike in its regularity but muffled. Also, there were other sounds in the rhythm of a chant.

As the seeking root writhed away from them, bearing its growing glow, a second one threw itself out, or was so thrown from some perch in the dark, whipping across the floor as if meant to sweep them from their feet. Kelsie lashed out the chain of the stone which was now a sullen shadow of itself. That also landed fair enough to send the root rope out of their way.

She tried to concentrate on the gem as she had in the pen but she could not summon up the same sure power she had known then. There was only a die-away spurt or two. Yet that appeared to be enough to keep the roots at bay. She wondered if Yonan knew where they were going. As far as she could judge he was heading on, straight into the dark. Again it was as if he could read her fatigue-deadened mind.

"There is an opening ahead. Taste the air—" She could see in the faint light from jewel and sword his tongue tip showing then between his lips as if he did in truth test so the fetid atmosphere. And she copied his gesture.

There *was* something! It was almost as if she had been offered a cup of water in the midst of all the fumes and heat of this dark place. The girl could see that her companion kept his tongue so as he urged her forward. Some of her strength seemed to return as she went until she could pull away from him and walk forward on her own.

The steady thunk-thunk of the distant drums and a hissing noise filled this place and she could hear voices rise and fall until it seemed that she could sort out the direction from which those came—to her right. The root ropes kept pace with them and now one or another, or sometimes two together would try once more to entangle their former captives. Though it appeared that Yonan need only show them the Quan on his sword hilt for them to flinch back.

Kelsie became aware that the stone under their feet was sloping upward and once she was sure she caught sight of a pale streak of light before them. Then came a sudden silence. The drums and the voices ceased, even the hissing of the root ropes faded away. She tongue-tried the air again—

The freshness was still there but in her nostrils was an ever growing taint of filth and damp and other odors she could not put name to. There might be an entrance somewhere ahead as Yonan believed but there was also a menace in between.

She gathered the stone swinging on its chain into the tender flesh of her hand and held it against her forehead. There was no reason that she could have told for that gesture, it simply seemed the right thing to be done.

Though her eyes were fastened upon the darkness ahead, there appeared in her mind another picture—that of a packed mass of the misshapen creatures she had only half glimpsed in the fire-lit ruin of the cage. To the fore were three who pounded with misshapen fists on the flat surface of bowl-like instruments they held between their knees. While the tooth-filled jaws of all showed as they sang no—called! Called upon what or whom? Kelsie shrank from knowing but she did not break the touch between her forehead and the jewel.

There was a swirl of reddish-yellow just before them drawing in upon itself, curdling into something far more sturdy than the mist from which it was born. Kelsie had expected a face, even a full figure, but what she saw was a sign which was a mixture of dots and lines, a pattern which reached outward for her own mind—offering more danger than the burning cage. She let the jewel fall forward but not before she gained a firm belief that that which had set the pattern had also been aware of her, and that they were far from being free from the hands of the servants—Thas—or perhaps even other and more powerful aides.

Only Yonan continued to walk steadily ahead and she saw that his attention was all for the Quan iron as if that could act as a scout and give them warning. Was the stone equal—

It flamed and the heat of that flare made her let it slide from out her fingers to dangle again. There were no roots this time to come slithering out of the dark. Rather she saw the light of her jewel mirrored in a mass of pairs of red points on the floor—eyes—?

"Rasti," Yonan broke the silence which had held between them.

Though there was a river of those eyes near the floor, it did not spread or try to engulf them as she had feared that it might. It would seem that these other dwellers in the dark were now as wary of them as the Thas had become. Yet, though they stopped their advance, they milled about, covering the rock between the two and what might be a door to the outer world. In experiment the girl swung out her jewel to the full length of its chain and noted that there was a wavering of the line in answer to that.

There sounded a shrill tittering call, rising sharply above the thumping of the bowl drums. The flood of the rasti parted, leaving a lane down which came something greater than the Thas, taller, stronger, and, Kelsie recognized by the instant repulsion in her, far more evil.

The yellowish light which had flowed from the stakes flared up once more spreading out from a rod that newcomer held. By its light the girl could see a figure as tall as Yonan, one which wore no armor, nor indeed any clothing at all, except patches of shaggy hair.

It pranced rather than strode, as if it were weaving a spell now by some unknown ritual. The crooked, hairy legs ended in hooves which were split for half their length. And those in turn kicked out at the rasti, striking home now and again against one of the animals to send it chittering and whirling off to thud against its fellows.

The rest of the figure was crooked of back as if it could not, because of its breadth and thickness of shoulder straighten to full height. Its belly protruded obscenely and altogether it was a daunting creature.

But above that crook-backed, flatulently-bellied body there was a head and that was as startling as if two separate creatures had been bound by some disgusting spell into a single form. For the head was perhaps neither male nor female, but it was that of great beauty with flawless features and masklike calm. While the hair which wreathed it was not the coarse stuff it grew elsewhere but a silken fall, brilliantly red in the light.

Strangest of all Kelsie discovered was the fact that it walked with closed eyes but not with the hesitation of something blinded, rather as if its body obeyed one set of rules which did not even reach behind the lowered eyelids.

She felt movement beside her. Then Yonan was facing the thing, with his shoulder before hers, as if to push her back and away from danger. The jewel was flaring up again and she could feel its drain on her own resources of spirit.

"Ah, Tolar that was—you have become over brave in these days. Or have you forgotten Varhum during your years of exile?" Those perfectly-formed lips moved extravagantly as the creature spoke and the lid-blinded eyes were clearly turned toward Kelsie's companion.

"Tolar is dead—long since," Yonan answered sullenly. "I do not remember."

"You mortals," the head shook a fraction and the voice was almost humorous. "Why do you so fear what is offered you? You were Tolar and perhaps the better for it, when last we met. That you must wait to be born again is the whim of the Great Power. But to refuse to remember, ah, Tolar, that is foolish. Varhum's walls were breached by—"

"Plasper forces," Yonan interrupted harshly. "And you are—"

"The eyes and mouth, and sometimes the weapon of one greater than you of the Light can even guess. Yet was I also once of your blood and kind."

There was a moment of silence, even the chittering of the rasti had stopped. Kelsie was aware of a shudder through her companion's body so close did they stand now.

"At Vock—?" It sounded like a question rather than the naming of a place.

Now the perfect lips curled in a small cruel smile. "Excellent! You see when you put yourself to it you can remember! Try no tricks to hide memory, Tolar. You know who I am in truth— Call my name if you dare after speaking of Plasper.''

Again Kelsie felt Yonan's shudder. But what she could see of his face remained as unchangeably calm as did that other's.

"Lord Rhain."

"Yes. And there were other names they called me that day, were there not? Traitor, Betrayer, Dark One! In your sight I was all those, was I not? But you see I have grown in wisdom—though that was the beginning of such wisdom— when I realized that we were swords for the wrong side— when Kalrinkar had the strength of the future with him. And so—" those crooked shoulders shrugged and again the small smile was shaped by the lips alone, "I lived—"

"In such a guise!" burst out Yonan.

"Do I properly afright you, once comrade? If I wish—" from the mouth came a curl of smoke which grew longer and denser, curling around that misshapen figure to hide it from sight, though Kelsie was very certain that it was still there. There was a small puff of yellow-red and the smoke was gone. In place of the hairy, bloated body which had confronted them was a straight limbed, nearly majestic man whose frame now fitted well his fine head and handsome features. Kelsie had the idea that this was certainly all illusion. Yet he was as real seeming now as he had been moments earlier in the half-bestial disguise.

"You see," even his voice had a different lilt, one far more human, lacking the subtle contempt the other had held, "I am truly Rhain—"

However, Yonan shook his head slowly. "You *were* Rhain. Now what are you to the eyes of those who stand by the Light?"

On impulse Kelsie, though again she could not have said why she did it, swung out the Witch Jewel by its chain. The bluish beam which had continued to emit now touched the tall, perfect body of he who confronted them. There was a fluttering in the air, almost as if some delicate glass had shattered and what she saw was the grotesque body come back into place while Yonan said loudly:

"Even our eyes you cannot bespell now, in spite of what you once were—"

But Rhain's attention had swung from the man he claimed as a former comrade to Kelsie and now there was as ugly a look on his face as to match his body.

"Witch!" he spat and a droplet of moisture hit the ground between them. "So you serve a female now, Tolar—you who were once your own man? Little do they repay those who march for them, being no true womenkind but only wills to rule. And you, witch, you shall find here that which you stake your life upon will have but little value. Long since Escore learned its secrets and powers which your kind may only have dreamed of dimly."

Power—into her from the jewel there was a warm flow— the draining she had felt so before was reversed. She began to walk slowly forward, edging around Yonan, then conscious that he had fallen in step with her. She raised her hands heart high at the breast and between steadied the jewel awkwardly, then more skillfully, as she sensed that what she was doing was right and meant to be. She fastened her will on the gem and once more reversed the flow, giving back to it what it had given her.

She heard dimly and then shut firmly out of her mind the chittering of the rasti who had milled around their master's feet, beyond that came the muffled sound of drumming where the Thas must have still lingered. But what held her mind and body was concentration on the jewel, rejoicing in the flaring up of its brilliance, in spite of the weakness it was leaving within her.

He who named himself Rhain, for all his brave words, fell back before her each step of hers being equaled by one of his retreat. His handsome face twisted more and more into a scowling pattern and now he hunched his crooked shoulders and shuffled his hooved feet as he fell back.

He gave a cry and she was aware of surge of the rasti but

she dared not drown the beam of the jewel. It was Yonan who swept forward with his sword, keeping clear the space before her. And Rhain cried out again, this time louder, more demanding.

Out of the dark came the living roots of the Thas—out to shrivel into nothingness as the gem light beat upon them.

"This is the best you can do, my lord?" Yonan's voice was both harsh and calm. "You who once commanded the Host? Your vermin are sadly less than that."

Rhain flung back his head and from his throat there came a roar as might be given by some great tormented cat. In Kelsie's hand the gem trembled and for the first time the steady beam of its radiance blinked.

Nine

There was a whirling in the air itself, a thickening of shadows. Still something within Kelsie held her to that advance and she kept her eyes on the man-beast before her. It seemed that he tried again and again to meet the flaming of the jewel squarely but could not hold his gaze. His hands raised as if to shut off the beam from his face, yet never did his lidded eyes open. While from his twisted mouth spilled grating sounds, as ugly in their way as his body.

The whirling of the air condensed into shadowy forms, manlike, yet she could glimpse them only from the corners of her eyes, for her gaze held on Rhain. Even as he chanted so did Yonan begin to answer with one oft repeated phrase.

One of Rhain's arms was held a-high as if he would urge on liege men into battle. She heard above his chant the rising squeals of the rasti. A wave of small dark forms rolled on, yet where the shine of the jewel was they appeared to shrivel into small black patches as if eaten up by fire.

Once more Rhain flung up his head and shouted—this time no rush of ritual words but what Kelsie guessed was a name. He might have called upon aid as a last resort.

The whirling shadows thickened, stood on the flooring of the cavern. Men, armed, battle-ready, each with weapon in hand and moving in with no care for the rasti whose bodies they spurned or overtrod.

There was the sweep of a mighty blow by axe at her head. She did not have time to twist or duck. Only the blade sheered away before it crashed against her. And to her right she heard a clash of metal against metal as Yonan at last found something solid he could attack. Yet still, moved by the will of the stone (for it seemed to her that that gem strove to make of her a servant, not tried to serve her) Kelsie advanced and Rhain withdrew step by unwilling step.

Then—

He was gone like a blink of eye, a shatter of lightning. With him vanished the shadow warriors. Only the rasti remained and from the dark behind came still the beat of the Thas bowl drums. But Kelsie knew as if it had been shouted aloud, that the strength of the attack had departed from them and way to escape was open—for the present. That Rhain or those who might control him had finished with them—that she did not believe. More than anything she wanted the fresh air of the surface, to be out in the open where there would be honest light of day or of moon and no more of this burrows. For with Rhain gone she was suddenly drained and stumbled, keeping her feet with an effort. Then she was aware of a strong arm behind her shoulder, the support of Yonan even though he needs must still swing sword to keep off the rasti.

So they wavered together up to a place where there had been a fall of stone and earth and from a hole above there shone the beams of the sun. In her hands the jewel glow died and was gone and she slung the chain back around her throat as she began to scrabble for a hold in that earth slide, to be out of this place of strange meetings and crawling fear.

It was Yonan's aid which brought her up and out and then they clung to one another as if, should they loose that grip, they would fall prey to the weakness in them. The man started to waver forward, dragging her with him, steering her around two great fallen stones spotted with an ugly orange-yellow fungus.

Then they were free and before them was a stand of brush by the roots of which flowed a trickle of water so clear that one could see the clustered stones on the sand of the runnel which contained it. She sank away from him, unable now to move one step before the next, and plunged her face into that water thrice over to wash away the remnants of the stench and the dust of the underground. She saw that Yonan had knelt beside her one hand cupping water to his lips, his other still on the sword lying bare now between them, his eyes sentry wise on all which lay about them.

Refreshed and somewhat more in command of herself, Kelsie looked back. The entrance to the underground world was centered in a scatter of fallen stone. Again her memory leaped to that similar ruin on the Scottish hillside. Had they come through another gate?

"Where are we?" she asked in a half whisper which seemed to be all she could voice at that moment.

She saw a trace of frown beneath his helm where it crossed above his brows. He arose and turned slowly, pivoting where he stood. Then he raised his sword and pointed to a way on her right.

"That is Mount Holweg. And this is to the north. We may have come farther than the Valley patrols have ridden. The shadow lies always north and east."

She sat where she was, considering him. Before this venture had begun he had been only one of the men who had been soldier sentries for the Valley. He was younger than Simon Tregarth and slighter. Yet she did not doubt that in his way he was as expert at this game of weapons and spells as the man she had first met—that other displaced from her own world. Only she wondered, now that she had time to think about his relationship to the monstrosity they had confronted in the tunnels below, about his past. At least he had been able to assure her of one thing—that they had not gone through another gate—back there among the fallen stones.

"He knew you—" she began abruptly, determined to make what sense she could of those words they had exchanged below.

To her surprise her companion shook his head.

"He knew Tolar." There was a straight line to his mouth, a slight forward jut of his chin as if he were fronting an enemy once more. "I am not Tolar—"

"Then why—?"

For the first time he stopped his roving survey of the world around them and spoke directly to her:

"It seems that a man can be born again even if he has passed the last gate of all. I have some proof that perhaps I was once one Tolar who fought the Dark in the long ago— and lost. If that be so then perhaps this life is a chance to right the swing of the scales and be another man. For, I swear it by my name giving, I am Yonan, and not he who went down to defeat then—"

"But you remember—" Kelsie dared not deny that anything was possible in this world. "You called that . . . that thing by name!"

"I remember . . . upon occasion," he agreed somberly, and then changed the subject with a swift question.

"Can you journey on, Lady? We are still too near to that!" He was reaching down one hand to pull her up to her feet, his bared sword still in his other so he used his chin to point to that unwholesome appearing tangle of fallen blocks through which they had come.

"Yes!" All at once she was remembering, too, not distant times but the rasti and the Thas. The one who named himself Rhain was gone with his shadow army, but surely the creatures he had left behind were just as deadly in their own way. However, could she go on? The gem had so drained strength out of her that she wondered if she could keep her feet to reach even the first tree of a small copse which lay in the direction they now faced.

She made it, accepting only now and then the grasp of his hand on her arm. Though the water of the stream had revived her in part she was aware now of a great hunger and her temples throbbed with the pain of a headache as if she had striven at some task which had been nearly at the limit of her strength.

"Where do we go?" she asked then. "I don't think I can go far."

His still bared sword pointed to some small plants growing in between the trees toward which he had been urging her.

"That is illbane. Even a power hunter of the Left Hand Way would avoid such as that. We can lay up in their protection until—" his voice trailed away and she asked more sharply:

"Until what? Do we head back toward the Valley with your mountain as a guide?"

"Can you go?"

His return question startled her and then she remembered the compulsion which had sent her in the beginning on this trail across an unknown country thick with danger. Deliberately she turned to face the distant mountain. There were the beginning banners of sunset forming to the west but she had no thought of starting out to retreat in the dark.

Kelsie took one step and then another, instantly aware of the movement of the gem which had begun a swing from right to left across her breast. Rising in her was still that need for pressing on, not backward to such safety as there might be in this country, but rather on in the opposite direction.

Reaching up she strove to take the chain into her fingers, to tear it away, throw it behind her. But her hands shook and she could not get grip which would serve. That chain might have been well greased the way it slipped away from her attempted hold.

"Can you go back?" Yonan had stopped at the edge of the copse to which he had guided her. He was behind her but no more than a sword length so. For that was all the space she had won.

"No!" Once again she tried to free herself from the chain, the gem of which was growing hotter so that she could feel its warmth through her clothing. A punishing warmth which would allow her no mercy.

"I can't. It won't let me!" Kelsie felt a rise of anger in

her hot against the stone, against Yonan, against all this world which had so entrapped her.

"Then let us to such shelter as there may be," he sounded impatient and she turned again ready to burst forth with bitter words. He was already showing his back to her, intent upon advancing along the line of those plants he had named a most powerful weapon against the Dark which they knew. She had seen dried stalks of illbane, crushed leaves, kept carefully in the Valley—the greatest resource a healer could harvest.

It was Yonan who was harvesting the plants now. He had taken off his plain helm, shedding with it the under cap of mail with its swinging strips to be pulled across the face before battle. His hair, curled down upon his forehead, was dark with sweat, though he was much lighter of countenance than the other men she had seen. Now he grasped a handful of leaves, crushing them between palm and fingers and then raising the mass to smear across his forehead leaving traces of thick green behind its passing.

Not knowing what he was doing but that it might just relieve some of the pain of her aching head, the weariness of her body, Kelsie followed his example. The sharp clean scent of the bruised leaves did clear her head from the last remaining memory of the stench of the underworld and she felt more alert, firmer of purpose than she had when she had come out into the open.

Yonan carefully plucked two larger leaves from another plant and wrapped the wad of herb within those, putting it in the pouch at his belt. And Kelsie again followed his example.

The trees of the copse were not too close together as to refuse them a way, though they needs must twist and turn for opening wide enough that they might get through. But they broke out at last into a circle of open land around which the copse appeared to form a wall. Yonan had sheathed his sword and Kelsie wished for their packs which lay behind somewhere in the Thas burrows. Her hunger had grown and she could see not even any berries which would take the edge off that growing pain.

"What do we eat?" she asked Yonan. After all he was far more used to tramping the countryside. He took out not his sword but a long knife and went to the nearest of the walling trees on the trunk of which there was a growth of green-brown stuff as big as his hand. Carefully he hacked the parasite loose from its support and then divided it into halves, holding one out to her. She hesitated and heard him say:

"It is fogmot—and can be eaten. Men have lived on worse in these lands." As if to encourage her by deed as well as speech, he raised the half of the mass he held to his mouth and bit into it.

Kelsie was too hungry by now to deny his assertion. The thing had a hard rind, but once that was broken the inside was as crisp as a full-fleshed apple. It was tasteless, as if she chewed and swallowed a soft chunk of wood. But a very little, just the portion he had given her, appeared to satisfy her hunger. She wanted no more of it.

Yonan had finished his part of the supply first and was now prowling around the edge of the clearing into which they had come. He had resumed his helm and there was an air of a sentry about him. Kelsie licked the last fragment of the food stuff from her lip and asked:

"Do we camp here?"

She noted his actions more carefully and saw that he had advanced his sword a few inches out of its sheath and was pointing that toward the wood. She studied her gem. The faint glow showed that the power within it was still alive but it had not awakened as it did when there was some menace awaiting them.

"It is safe," he said as he took the last steps which had made the circuit of the tree wall complete. "In fact—" He strode to the center of that circle and swung his sword hilt around, arm's length above the grass of the turf. There was an answering gleam in the Quan inlay, and, as he thrust the sword point into the ground at that point, the blue flashed even higher. "This is a sanctuary," he said. "Try it with your jewel."

This time the chain did not resist her touch or slip through her fingers. She came close to where he stood and held the gem between her fingers. There was a noticeable gleam of life which came in answer.

"There are such places," he said more as if he were reassuring himself than explaining something to her. "And many exist near points of danger—though which came first—the blessed place or that of the Dark we do not know."

He dropped down to sit on his heels his sword once more in sheath. She confronted him settling cross-legged on the ground.

"So we are in a blessed place," she said challengingly. "But we cannot carry it with us and—"

What she would have added to that complaint was lost in a howl which arose to blanket hearing of anything but that long wavering cry. Kelsie clutched the stone to her and felt the heat of its full awakening. There was a second howl from a different quarter, answering the first eagerly.

She had heard their like before. That hound which had been set upon the gate place by the rider. Were they to be under siege again and this time so far from any help from the Valley as to be easily taken?

Yonan was plainly listening. It was near twilight now and shadows which had gathered under the trees were creeping out into the open where they were. A third howl and that from yet another direction! A pack of the creatures ringing around.

"Will . . . will they come here?"

"I think not," Yonan returned. "This is a blessed place, remember. Curses and blessings grow thin through the years but that which was set here answered to us. That we may be able to go forth again—that is another matter." His expression was set and grim and Kelsie shivered. To be pent in this place, no matter how safe it might be at its core was no way to stay. She watched Yonan, on his feet once more, sword out digging point into the tough rooted turf.

Soil and clods of grass flew. Was he trying to *dig* his way out? Kelsie shrank back and away, having no thought of landing below ground once again. Then she heard the sword point grate on a surface below and Yonan's efforts to clear what lay there speeded up. He was so intent that Kelsie thought he would not even hear her if she asked what he was doing.

He hacked and dug and then dropped on his knees, putting aside his sword and using his knife and his hands to continue. What he uncovered so was a star of white stone, large enough for a person to stand upon. Now Yonan was working more cautiously, shifting the soil away by handfuls, using knife point to dig out some stubborn clay which clung to depressions and cracks in the artifact.

"What is it?" Kelsie could contain her curiosity no longer. Why her companion thought it necessary to do this while the forces of the Dark gathered beyond the trees, and already evening shadows grew thicker and thicker, she did not understand.

There was a hole in the center of the star which he was clearing with care. Now he picked up his sword and dropped its point into that aperture. It was as if he had whirled a smoldering torch into life. From the Quan in the hilt streamed light which filled half the clearing with the brightness of day.

From overhead came a rasping sound and the rush of wings through the air. But nothing she could see cut the light of the sword. If the enemy had forces aloft they were not tempted to strike now.

"What was that?" Kelsie's question was now a demand.

Yonan looked at her across the flare of light. It seemed to her that his eyes blazed as had the hounds' when she had taken refuge in that other place of power—yet the sight did not revolt her as it had before.

"I have seen one other like this," he answered somewhat obliquely. "It is a gathering place for power. If we had the old knowledge we could take that," he waved toward the now blazing sword where up and down the blade ran runnels of light, "and win through any force which has been set against us here. But," he pounded his fist against his knee in open bafflement, "we know so little!"

It had brought his sword to life, what would it do for the Witch Jewel? On impulse the girl pulled the chain from about her neck and dangled the gem over the star. There was an explosion of light. Into her fingers, her arm, her shoulder, her whole body shot a flash of strength so powerful that she was hurled backward on the turf, thus involuntarily jerking the jewel out of line of the star. That inflow of energy stopped but the gem still blazed. Could this be the place Wittle had been seeking, where the old power could be summoned to enhance witch weapons?

Yonan's hand closed about her wrist, pulling back and down the hand which held the gem chain.

"Do not summon that!" his voice held the snap of an order. "You do not know what you may control or what may be beyond your knowledge of use."

He was right, of course, but she resented his interference. She had not spoken against his use of the sword.

"A key," it was as if he could read her mind. "The sword is the key. Now," he had not released his hold upon her but tightened it, setting his strength of body against hers before she could understand what he would do and resist having a part in it.

So did he draw her to her feet and forward also in a single movement so that she was treading upon the star stone itself. Quivers of energy vibrated in his body. She would have thrown herself back and away but not only Yonan held her there, this was part of the power they had aroused and it kept her motionless. Yonan reached out, his other hand gripped the sword firmly, and he called aloud in a shout which reached above the baying of the hounds.

"Ninutra!"

There was a hush as the echoes of his shout died away.

The hounds howled no longer. Kelsie quivered with expectancy. What now had he summoned?

"Ninutra! Hilarion!" Now he had added a second name to the first.

There was a haze rising from the points of the star as if lamps or candles were sending forth a smoke which was of light not of dark. Each of those streams inclined inward and now they veiled the very center of the copse beyond the star. Yonan's grip on her had not loosened, instead it had tightened to a bruising ring of fingers leaving nail marks on her flesh. Under the shadow of his helm his eyes were closed, there was a strain on his features as if he dared now some deed beyond which he dared not even look.

"Ninutra!"

The sword blazed high, flames wrapped about his hand and arm but he did not loose his hold. The whirl of the mist tongues about them made Kelsie feel faint and ill. She closed her eyes. Then came a blast of cold, a feeling of such terror that she could not even voice a scream of protest. They were lost in some place where her kind was never meant to travel. Yet there was a power that whirled them on—and on—and on. She clung to that, fearing to be left alone in this place above all.

Then—dark—complete and terrible darkness—and still the power held them—

It was gone—they were lost in this—this—

"Kelsay! Kelsay!"

She was blind, she was sick, she was lost—

"Kelsay?"

She was so overcome by weariness and weakness that it required a major effort to raise her eyelids and see now that the dark was not complete. Yonan's face with the moon streaking across it was close to hers. She was in his arm still though she lay upon stone, his hold, rock steady, bringing her up against his chest.

"Kelsay—we are out!"

The words meant nothing for a long moment of time. Part

of her seemed still caught and held by that nothingness which had been. Then behind his head she saw what was certainly not the tree wall of the grove but instead what could only be a wall of stone, dappled by the moonlight shifting through holes.

She drew a deep breath and then another. On her breast was a warm pulsing and she did not need to feel for it to know that it was the gem.

"Where—where are we?" Her voice was a weak whisper.

He drew her up higher against him so she could see more. Beside him lay the sword no longer a-ripple with power but still a small beacon of light. Kelsie could see now more walls and overhead the night of moon and stars. It was plain that wherever they were it was not the copse in which they had been besieged.

"Where are we?" He echoed her question. "I do not know—save that we are away from those who nosed so closely on our trail. This was once a mighty keep, I think." He was looking about, too, as if trying to see what had once stood complete and formidable.

"But how did we get here?" she asked quickly. It would be a long time before she would forget that passage through the Other Place where her kind went at great peril as she was now aware.

"We had a key; we used it—" His hand went out again to the hilt of his sword. "A year agone Urik found such a path when the gray ones had him at their mercy, or so they thought. The old ones had their own ways of travel which are not ours except when the choice may be certain death behind."

Ten

Their new shelter had nothing of the stench of the Thas caverns, nor of the indescribable odor which had filled the copse from which they had been so strangely snatched. It was dark, save where the moon struck through rents in the walls, and very chill. So that the two of them huddled together for the sheer need of bodily warmth. Nor did they sleep, but dozed and awoke and dozed again until the gray of early morning showed them more clearly where they had come.

The walls of the place might have been laid by giants for there were great blocks fitted together with no sign of securing mortar—rather as if their weight alone, once they were in place, were enough to cement them for all time. These formidable barriers extended well up. Above was rubble less expertly laid, much of which had cascaded down into the great room where they were sheltering. By the revealing light of day Kelsie could see that they had spent the night in the center of another great star many times the width of that which Yonan had uncovered but fashioned in the same way. Between the points were symbols engraved on the pavement. One of those recalled a memory for Kelsie—of Wittle sketching a like pattern in the air.

Yonan was a-foot, first going to the nearest wall and

jumping until his hands caught on the rougher stone above. Then by a feat of strength he was able to pull and work himself up, sending small cascades of ancient stones sliding down in a cloud of dust.

"Where are we?" Kelsie had turned around to survey the place of the star. That had been fashioned close to the wall, but there stretched out a large segment of space beyond. She could see no ground entrance to this room—only the walls about.

Yonan balanced, slowly turning his head from side to side, working his way around on the treacherous coating of the upper wall so that he could see at least three-quarters of what lay beyond.

"A keep . . . I think . . ." he was plainly uncertain. "But a very old and long since deserted one. There are such to be found, though usually we avoid them. But with that," he nodded at the star in which she still stood, "I do not think that this is any trap of the Dark. Look to your jewel—does it blaze in warning?" He held onto his perilous perch with one hand and with the other sought the hilt of his sword. There was a warmth in her stone but no fire and she reported as much.

He nodded. "The power is very old here—near exhausted and—" His head swung suddenly around and she could see his body tense.

"What is it?" She had moved now to the wall directly below his perch.

He made a silencing gesture with his hand. It was plain to Kelsie that he was listening, listening and staring beyond to seek the source of whatever it was he heard.

Now she concentrated on hearing, too. There was a distant bark—but it did not have the fierce threat of a hound's cry. Then, from the air, sounded a trilling which was far from the hoarse cries of the dark flying things which companied those of the Dark.

From Yonan's own lips came a whistle, close in pattern to the trill. Kelsie saw the flash of rainbow wings, the light body those carried. There hung in the air before her companion one of the flamen, the small humanoid body supported by the fast flutter of the wings. She had seen them often in the Valley and knew what was told of them, that they were capricious and short of memory—they might carry messages but could easily be turned from their task by something else new which caught their attention.

Now it landed near to Yonan, its wings only half folded, as if it would make off in an instant, peevish at being controlled even by so little as answering his signal. He whistled again, his face set in a mask of impatience.

Kelsie was as aware of the hostility of the flyer as much as if it had cried aloud denial of having to have anything to do with the two. There was a coaxing note in Yonan's whistle and then he spoke rapidly in a series of singsong words she could not recognize.

The flamen shook its head violently, gave an upward bound which carried it out into the air and almost instantly beyond Kelsie's range of sight. Yonan whistled twice more but it did not return.

"Not of the Valley," there was a disappointed note in his voice. "It is one of the unsworn. Which means—" He fell silent.

"Which means what?" she demanded, when he did not continue.

"That we have come far eastward—perhaps well beyond all the trails known to the Valley people."

"Can you still see your mountain?"

He shifted carefully about and searched the air so far above her. "That may be it. But . . . there are leagues now between—" He was facing at an angle to the room below.

She waited for that touch of buried compulsion which always in her answered any thought of returning to what safety this land could offer. Yes, it still rode with her even now. Without thinking she, too, turned to face in near the opposite direction from Yonan's stance. Whatever drew her lay still ahead in the unknown.

However, when she spoke it was of more immediately practical things.

"We need food and water—" Both hunger and thirst were making themselves known now.

"Come up!" He lowered himself to his belly and reached down his hands. She gave a jump and felt fingers catch one of her wrists while her other hand missed and scrabbled at the stone until he managed to seize it also. He was stronger than he looked, this warrior of the Valley, for somehow, with very little assistance from her, he brought Kelsie up beside him on the crumbling top of the wall.

What stretched for a distance before her and on every side were more walls marking rooms, or passageways, long unroofed. In addition the pile stood on a mound or small hill, and stretching out from that was a patchwork of fields each also partitioned by broken walls. There was an opening not far to their left which suggested a road had led here and that that maze of rock had been the entrance to this place. But nowhere was there any hint of water.

"That way—" Yonan pointed north and rose to his feet cautiously. His motion, as wary as it was, started a slip of loose stone down into the room of the star.

"There are no doors." Kelsie had noted that almost at once. These walls sealed in each room one from the other, and their only path to freedom appeared to be by the tops of those shaky divisions.

"That is the truth. Therefore we must take these upper ways and with full care. Follow me, and, if you can, place your feet where mine have been."

The sun was up and beginning to warm the rocks about them before they reached that point which once might have been a gate. Not only was Kelsie hungry and thirsty but she was also trembling from the tension of that journey. Twice they had had to make detours which had lost them much time because the wall tops were too unsteady to allow them footage.

Though she looked with hope into each room they passed

she saw no way of going except by this dangerous path they had chosen. There were no doorways, no trace of any floor side opening from one space into the next. This amazed her.

"They might have had other means of entrance," Yonan commented when she spoke of this. "If they were winged for example."

"Flamen!" she burst out in denial. She could not think of the small airborne creatures as the architects of such massive walls.

"There may be—or were once—other flyers beside the flamen," he told her soberly. "It is well known that the adepts played with the very forces of life itself, creating new creatures for their own use or amusement. Such are the Krogan, the water people, and even the Thas. There were few of true blood left when the rest of the Old Ones thought to flee such unnatural dealings and went into Estcarp, laying upon themselves forgetfulness of their land lest they be tempted to so misuse the power again. But whoever set these stones together are now long gone. Ah, take this wall, and then that, and we shall be at outer bailey at last."

Perforce she followed him, though the footing was never safe and she tottered on the edge of slipping twice before they reached the point he indicated and could look down at the earth below.

Yonan selected a portion of the wall path which appeared to show the least of time's erosion and lay flat on it. Then he ordered Kelsie:

"Give me your hands and swing over. You will drop but I think that the space is not so much we cannot make it. We have no other choice."

There was a drop certainly and she hit ground, to roll over the edge of another small fall, coming to stop painfully against one of those broken field walls. There was a whir in her face which made her start and cry out as two birds took off out of a clump of grass before her, not ascending very high into the air but covering a goodly space before they alit and disappeared again into the tall cover of the field.

When Yonan joined her he was fumbling with his sword belt and produced a length of what looked like tough cord, a small weight fastened to either end.

"Circle," his command was delivered in a voice hardly above a whisper, and he motioned with his hand toward where the birds had taken again to cover. "Come at them from the south if you can, but get them up."

She obeyed in spite of her bruises, trying to walk as noiselessly as she could through the vegetation which was waist-high grass, giving support here and there to a loaded seed head as if it were some form of wild sown grain.

There was another whir and eruption of feathered bodies. Something whirled through the air and one of the birds fell, entangled foot to wing by Yonan's weighted cord. A moment later he passed her in a leap, knife in hand, and used that expertly to put an end to the wildly struggling bird.

Following the same method of hunt they added two more of the low-flying prey to their first capture. Then Yonan, swinging the birds by their feet, turned aside from the open into an ancient field where the stones at one corner had shifted forming a small half cave. He went to work at once, skinning and gutting the birds, saying:

"Get some dry wood." He jerked one hand toward where a straggle of trees stood. This once might have been an orchard, Kelsie decided, but only one or two of the trees showed any signs of life by ragged greenery. Some storm of the past had laid others low and she went among those breaking off branches and carrying an arm load to where Yonan was conducting his bloody business.

She watched him lay a fire of sticks hardly more than twigs and then light those with a stone from his belt pouch struck against his knife until sparks flew into a handful of grass in the center of his cave oven.

"This will break the smoke," he told her as he worked and she felt that he was deliberately sharing with her information which was the result of long training at living off the land, a land which had nearly as many perils as blades of grass in the field. He had pieces of the birds spitted on trimmed branches and already over the fire while others were hung well out of the flames but where the smoke, partially trapped under the stones, could reach them.

He was right as that smoke emerged in wisps which drifted in different directions at the will of the breeze. Kelsie having built up a goodly supply of wood inspected more fully the seed heads in the field growth. She rubbed some free of their stems and between the palms of her hands, blowing away the chaff and being rewarded with a handful of what was unmistakably some form of grain. She tasted it, finding it chewable and slightly sweet. Then she set about gathering enough of it still on the stem to make an arm load. Though as she went she watched carefully what lay around.

More of the birds were dislodged from their feeding and flew clumsily perhaps as far as the next field. She could smell now the odor of the cooking meat and it drew her, though she wanted most of all a drink of water to rinse away the dryness of the grain she had eaten.

She returned to their improvised fireplace to find Yonan, his attention divided between the roasting meat and something he held before his hands to saw at with his knife. It was yellow in color and shaped not unlike a gourd of her own world, though larger than she had ever seen. Having chopped off its top he was now turning the knife around and around in its interior, shaking free at short intervals pieces of woodlike flesh hung with black seeds.

Kelsie saw that two more of the odd vegetables, if that is what they were, rested beside his knee. She pulled loose the scarf that had covered her head when she had set out from the Valley and began to rub into it the grain she had harvested. Yonan looked closely at what she had found and then nodded.

"Pound that into flour," he commented, "and with drippings from those—" he indicated the birds, "you will have a kind of journey cake."

"What about water?"

He slapped the gourd he was working on. "There is a spring in that last opening beyond where we came down. Did you not see the water reeds?"

She had to admit that she had not, her full attention being on how she could zigzag along the walls without a slip. However, he did not wait for her answer as he set aside the first of his gourds and inspected the meat, turning the spits on which the chunks were impaled with the familiarity of an expert at such cookery.

The meat was done to his satisfaction and laid on the large leaves which he had harvested from the same plant as bore the gourds. Then he took the first of those and stood up, looking at her appraisingly.

"Can you give me a foot up. It is over the wall for our water."

She was willing enough, her dry throat and mouth sending her to stand braced against the outer wall while he got himself to her shoulders. His punishing weight only lasting there for a moment before he was up on the wall.

The sun was already well toward that rippling black line which marked the horizon as she stood there, pressed to the rough stone, wondering how they could find any safe shelter for the coming night. That memory of the howling hounds and the black rider were very clear in her mind. They might have come to this ruin through some knowledge of another race but that did not mean that they were free of pursuit, and she had an idea that the creature Yonan had called by the name of a once man—Rhain—would not so tamely accept defeat.

Kelsie was fingering the chain of the jewel when she heard a scrambling on the wall top and jumped back away from a clatter of some broken pieces which heralded Yonan's return. He lowered to her by the aid of the same cord which had entangled the birds a gourd slopping water. It was so full she had to exert all her self-command not to hold it to her mouth and drink long and full. Then he was over and down beside her and said:

"Take small sips—" he waved away the gourd when she would have given it back to him, "small sips first."

Obediently she sucked in a mouthful and held it for a long moment of sheer delight before she swallowed. Yonan had brought something else with him, a bundle of reeds, and as they went back toward their fire and the waiting food he picked up two of the fallen stones, each of which fitted snugly into his hand. With these he began to crush the reeds, turning them swiftly into strings of fiber which he twisted tightly one to another until he had a lengthline of rough cord.

Night was now fully upon them and their small cooking fire had been purposefully allowed to dwindle to a near dead ash, the sparks sheltered from sight by more stones. Yet Yonan bent over his task by that smallest gleam of light and continued to work. When he had a length of the coarse and, to Kelsie, not-to-be-trusted stuff, he set up two sticks and began to weave between them back and forth methodically, more by touch than sight.

She sat cross-legged at the other side of their palm-sized fire and at last curiosity won:

"What are you doing?"

"We need a bag for that," with a shadow of gesture he indicated the meat they had so haphazardly smoked, "also we need shoes—"

"Shoes?" Startled her hand actually went to the half boots she was wearing. They were scuffed and perhaps scratched past all polishing but they were still intact on her feet. To throw such away for a rough mass of the stuff Yonan was playing with was the act of a fool and she bit her tongue to keep from saying so.

"The gray ones," he was continuing, "hunt by sight and scent together but the night hounds by scent alone. We shall give them such scenting as will send them off our trail for a goodly time."

He had laid to one side part of his rough weaving and now he moved his foot into the faint glow of light. From the pouch at his belt he took out the mass of illbane which he had harvested and began to rub it vigorously along the length of rope. When he had done he laid aside the mass of leaves and began to wind the rope around one of his own feet, shaping it back and forth until he was sure by touch that the entire metal-enforced boot sole was completely covered.

"That will help?" Kelsie wanted assurance, though she had begun to grasp what he would do.

"We can wish it so—illbane has many services. Now we shall test one of these."

Thus when they settled for the night, one to watch for a space and the other to sleep, their feet were encased in stringy reed and small bits of torn vegetation. The clean, clear smell of illbane was in her nostrils as Kelsie took first watch, allowing the fire to die into ash. The moonlight gave her the only sighting of the pile of the ruin and the fields about.

She listened in a queer fashion which combined both mind and body. It was like testing the air for a strange scent—that loosing of thought waves to pick up the first alert against anything the shadows might hide. What she waited for tensely was the howling of the hounds that ran for and with the Black Hunter and his like.

There was life a-stir in the night rightly enough. She picked up rustling in the tall grain, once a screech which brought her scrambling to her feet until she realized it must be the voice of some aerial hunter. But there came no howl, none of that crawling of the skin which she associated with the hounds. How far they were from that copse in which they had been besieged she could not begin to assess. If Yonan knew—which she suspected he did not—he never said. Though his established sentry watches for the both of them certainly argued that he saw little safety in their present position.

Sleep pulled at her. She got to her feet once in that battle against drowsiness and walked over stones where there was no grass rustle to betray her to the outer wall of the roofless keep. There she stood trying to imagine what manner of intelligent creature had built this pile with such strength and yet had made no door to enter, no passage of inner walls to follow from one room to another. It was as silent and as much a part of long hidden and forgotten history as that broken circle back on Ben Blair.

Ben Blair—with a sudden shiver of new fear Kelsie realized that Ben Blair was now so far from her life as to be a distant dream. She had questioned Simon Tregarth about return. He had been evasive but when she had insisted he had told her that to return through the gate one had come through was unknown. One could find other gates in this land and make use of them to go still farther into strange times and places, but to return to one's own proper place—

Proper place. She remembered now that Simon had said that hesitantly, and at last had told her that most of those using the gates had done so for escape. Their "proper places" had come to be in this world, which many had deliberately sought.

Well, she had not! And she wanted—

Looking at the black bulk of the ruin only half displayed in the moonlight, she tried to think of a gate here. If she went through where would she find herself? With something better or something worse? She cupped the witch stone in one hand and felt its comforting warmth. Then her thoughts were swiftly served by an urgency and she held the stone away from her to stare into its heart where there was light flickering and growing stronger. She had taken one step back toward where she had left Yonan, aware that there had been a change. But not from in the land about.

The light emitted from the stone curdled about it until, though she could still feel the warming jewel in her hand, she could not see anything but a seething ball of light. Imprinted on that was a shadow which became darker and more distinct with every beat of her heart.

"Wittle!" She breathed that name aloud and at its saying the reflection steadied. Kelsie was looking straight into the witch's eyes as if they stood face to face, and she felt the compulsion which had always been with her since she had taken up the stone become more than she could control.

In the light the witch's mouth opened. But it was not words that reached Kelsie, rather a straight beam of sharp and compelling thought.

"Where?"

Kelsie answered with the truth. "I do not know."

"Fool! Look about you! Lend me your eyes if you cannot answer straightly."

The pressure of that order was such that Kelsie found herself pivoting slowly, facing first the ruin, and then the fields before, back once again to the ruin.

Now the mist face expressed exasperation and certain vindictiveness against which Kelsie stiffened.

"Is the man still with you?" The accent on the word "man" made an expletive out of it.

Kelsie pictured Yonan asleep as she had left him moments earlier.

"Go while he sleeps then! Follow the jewel's note—it seeks the great power."

Kelsie shook her head firmly. "I leave no one in this land asleep and open to attack." From that stubborn inner part of her which had always resented Wittle she drew the strength to say that—say it or think it.

She saw the witch's eyes in full light, trying to hold hers, to compel her. But instead she dropped the jewel out of her hand, let it swing back against her breast. The bubble which it had formed vanished. Wittle for all her knowledge had been vanquished—for now. Only Kelsie was left with the feeling that had they confronted each other in truth she would not have so easily come out the better of the two. The more she used the stone—was compelled to use it—the more that feeling of inner strength grew in her. But she had no wish to become a witch—one like Wittle. It would seem that she was in some way subservient to the stone but she was still herself, not of a sisterhood who had come to focus on their gems the whole of their lives.

She went swiftly back down from beside the ruin to their camp. There was no way of telling time but the shadows reached farther into the valley about and she was sure that she must awaken Yonan. He, at least, was not under Wittle's influence and— She hesitated a moment—must she tell him of that meeting through the gem's powers? He might from that gain good reason to distrust her and she was certain that only with Yonan beside her did she have a chance of survival. This far it had been largely his knowledge and training which had brought them through.

Eleven

Kelsie need only touch Yonan's shoulder and he was instantly awake. His face turned toward hers and she realized that she would not tell of Wittle—since she had no intention of carrying out the witch's suggestion. Settling in his place on the mass of grass they had pulled for a bed she willed herself to sleep. But she had not willed herself to dream and she never knew whether it was the doing of the witch from Estcarp or her own imagination which straightway plunged her into one of the most realistic nightmares which had ever aroused her sleeping fears.

Kelsie was back in the room of the star into which they had entered so unceremoniously. But the walls were intact now and the star itself blazed on the floor as if drawn in lines of living fire. What crouched in the center of that field of protection was wholly alien. The thin gray-skinned body was hardly removed from a skeleton with skin and not flesh to cover the bones. Two leathery wings were half folded about that same body as a man or woman might pull a cloak.

However, it was the head and face of the creature which drew her full attention. The face was narrow, the nose more beak than just a nasal passageway and the chin retreated sharply. It was the eyes which dominated that sliver of countenance—huge and faceted as might be those of an insect, all seeing and—all knowing.

This was no servant of some adept who had pulled into this realm through his or her use of power. No, this was the adept! And that thing was aware of Kelsie for it swung swiftly around, the unreadable eyes turned on her.

In hands, which were more like the talons of some bird of prey than palms with fingers, it held a slender rod topped with a point of Quan iron burning as blue as did the helm of Yonan's sword. This it also swung until it was leveled straight at her.

The small mouth under that beak of nose twisted, open and shut, as if the thing were chattering some speech, question, or bit of ritual. Yet Kelsie did not hear with either mind or ear. Then she traced a shadow of expression on the avianlike face. The spear-wand arose and gestured through the air, leaving trails of blue smoke after it. And that smoke outlined what could only be a face.

A face and yet not a face. There was rigidity to it which more nearly suggested a mask, yet one far more human in appearance than the countenance of the creature which had summoned it. The mask slipped down, fitted itself over its creator. Now the creature arose and fanned its wings outward. Those were no longer dull grayish skin but rather formed a nebulous of light about a thoroughly human body and the creature was a woman.

Though the hands which held the rod might have changed, that weapon or trapping of power remained the same. Once more it traveled through the air and the curls of light which followed it straightened into a line moving out toward Kelsie.

Her wonder and beginning wariness was sharpening into fear. Though she was more than a little afraid of Wittle she could summon at least an outward stand against the witch. But this bird-woman was more than Wittle, Kelsie knew that instinctively. Whether she stood in the lines of the Dark or the Light there was no guessing for outward strangeness of body did not mean inward twisting of mind and belief.

Who—what—now claimed her?

There was warmth about her and Kelsie took heart from that for it seemed to her that with the evil always accompanied cold. Perhaps it was the jewel awakening to this other manifestation of the beyond-world.

"Far traveler—"

Into Kelsie's mind beat the words. It seemed part of a question. She was not aware of her physical body so she did not nod, only accepted the designation as the truth.

"Waker of the sleeping—"

"Not by my choice!" Out of her mind arose the answer.

"Back and back," continued that mind voice. "There was a choice and you were open to it—"

For a fraction out of time she stood again on Ben Blair and struck up the gun which was aimed at the already wounded wildcat. Was that the choice which had led to this?

"There was a choice," the winged one replied to her scrap of memory. "There have been others and will be more. You have dared one of the ancient ways, you will dare another—and yet another—"

"Do you wish me ill?" Kelsie sent that thought impulsively into the dream.

"For me there is no well nor ill. But you have evoked the power in a place where once it dwelt. Thus you have loosed yet more of the stuff of struggle. That long asleep stirs, be careful at how you welcome it, woman of another world. Be very careful."

The wand dipped its point, the illumination which made the figure look human failed, she saw again the gray skeleton, its beelike eyes trained upon her. There was a remoteness which was raising a wall between them. If she had had any thought of appealing to this other one for aid to come that fast withered and was gone. Neither of the Light nor of the Dark, this was one removed by choice from the battle. But who else was now awakened to what passed in Escore through Kelsie's and Yonan's intrusion?

"What will you do?" She dared to ask that now of the alien thing once more crouched within the blazing star.

She had an impression of cold amusement. "Ah, but that choice is mine. And I do not choose—"

The inner room of the ruin, the winged one, all of that vivid dream was gone in an instant. Instead there was darkness and a freezing cold. In that darkness something moved, leaned forward to observe her, something aroused from a lethargy which had lasted for ages. It would seem that here were balances. This thing she now fronted so blindly was the obverse of the winged thing. It did not try to communicate, it was merely fastening her in its mind, homing in upon her as a link with the world.

This was danger! Do not let it read her—stand against it! Her only weapon was the jewel. Still she hesitated to use it here. She stood within the boundaries of a place which was wholly inimical to all of her kind, and that which languidly and lazily observed her was something which she could not see—only feel the slimy touch of its curiosity.

Think of the jewel—no! She believed that that was the last thing she must do here and now. Think of—Ben Blair standing tall on another world—the world of easy life which was her own. Grimly Kelsie clung to her mind picture of the mountain, strove to recall its scents, its very being.

Was the thing in the dark deceived? She had no way of telling but she was drawn away from that place quickly and awoke, to find Yonan on his knees beside her, his hand on her shoulder as if he had physically pulled her out of that place of foulness and threat.

"You dream—" there was a tone in his voice which was faintly accusatory.

"You broke it!" She was aware of warmth, perhaps not of the night around her—the true night—but rather that of companionship. Since Yonan had joined them on the trek she had many times realized that his skills were what might bring them to whatever goal the jewel had imposed upon her. But this waking was one of the things which was even more to her service.

"We have awakened something by our passage," she told him with eager haste, wanting to share with another human, to free herself from that fear and that sense of being now linked to what she did not understand.

In the moonlight she saw him frowning. He flicked a finger at the jewel she wore, not quite touching it.

"Such a symbol may indeed call—"

Her first warmth faded. After all was it not his sword which had provided the key that had opened this door?

"Yours the key," she returned.

There was a flush on his face which she could see even by moonlight. At first she thought he was not going to answer, then he said:

"Each time we use power we may be troubling the scale. And the result may not include only us." His hand was on the Quan iron in his sword hilt. "You dreamed— or did you answer some call of another?"

She told him then—of the winged creature and then of that which had stirred in the darkness. At her story of that his mouth straightened and she saw his sword hand tighten.

"We go— This," he waved to the ruin, "is a focus through which they reached you. If we go—" But he had already turned to bind up their now scanty possessions. The slightly smoked meat he stowed in the coarse bag he had woven while he urged upon her the foot covers, awkward and hard to fasten.

There was a grayness along the horizon when they had made their simple preparations to be on the trail again. Yonan pointed to that distant northern peak which he had indicated before.

"If we take that as a mark—"

"A mark for what and to lead us where?" she countered, still dealing with the mass of reed which made such untidy bundles for her feet. "Back to the Valley?"

His face was set. "The Valley has its own protections but no place is invincible. We could lead that which watched you straight into the heart of that which must be protected above all. You say that your jewel leads us—very well—follow—"

"To draw danger after us!" No question but a protest. "If that is so, it is so."

She fired up at that. Who was this warrior who was willing to use her as bait to protect his own home? She had no need for loyalty to the Valley, her first thought should be her own peril. To wander through this cursed countryside was no choice of her own—but one she seemed to be forced into by ill luck, by being at the wrong place at a crucial time. All she wanted was to get back to Lormt. Lormt? To her mind she had never heard of that before. Yet she could close her eyes for a moment and see dim halls where ghostlike figures moved slowly as if bemused by their own surroundings.

Another dream or fragment of one—? Where was Lormt and why did she feel the need for reaching it again— Again? She had never been there!

No, but someone else had. Her lips shaped the name Roylane but she did not speak it aloud. By wearing the jewel did she also carry some frail remnant of the true owner with her now? Kelsie longed for someone she could trust enough to ask outright questions. Dahaun of the Valley might be such but they were far from the Valley and its co-ruler now.

"Where do you go?" she lengthened her stride to match step with Yonan. He answered her as curtly:

"It is more like where you go, Lady."

Her hand loosed on the jewel and it was warm. She pulled free its chain and allowed it to swing pendulum-wise from her middle finger. There was a scrap of memory, gone so fleetingly that she could not pin it down. So she had stood once before—no, not she—but that other.

Through no urging of her own the jewel began to swing—not in a circle as it had before, but rather back and forth, pointing outward and then to her. And the way it took was east. As firm footed as if she had been given an order she could not gainsay, Kelsie turned in that direction and began to walk, knowing indeed that bound as she was, there was only the gem in real control of their path.

There were bright banners of dawn in the sky as they walked along what might have once been a road between the ancient fields. Berries clustered on thorny branches which hung over tumbling walls and she did as Yonan, swept up what she could garner, stuffing them into her mouth. They were tart and sweet at the same time and she found them refreshing, but too few to give her a feeling of having truly breakfasted.

The forgotten road transversed the open until they came again to where stands of wood broke up the fields and grew closer and closer together until they faced another wood. A small animal with a dusky red coat broke for cover, was gone before Yonan could free with throwing cord, if he wished to hunt. And there were birds—not in flight but sitting on branches to watch them pass, twittering and calling, to be answered by others ahead as if their coming was being heralded to some feathered overlord whose domain this was.

They still had a way which had narrowed to hardly more than a footpath being overhung with brush and giving rooting to stubborn grass. Once Yonan flung out a hand to ward her from touching against a bush with singular ragged looking leaves and flowers of a dull green color which gave forth a thick and cloying scent.

"Farkill," he explained. "The odor is a sleep maker, to touch it raises ulcers on the skin, ones which even illbane finds hard to heal. And there," he pointed to a grim gray skeleton of a tree which set a little away from their path, "is also danger. Quick!" His arm fell about her shoulders so suddenly and heavily that she was swept from her feet as she heard a whishing in the air.

"Creep—on your belly," her companion ordered. "Do you want such as that in you?" he indicated a gray shaft which stuck, still quivering, in a bush at what might have been at the level of her shoulders had she still been on her feet.

It was in the shape of a thorn but as long as Kelsie's forearm and she gathered that it could have impaled her had it struck. In some manner it had been so shot by the dead-looking tree.

Creep indeed they did and she wrinkled her nose at the sour smell of the muck of long dead leaves which floored their path. Twice more they passed arrow trees until at last they came into the open once again, a glade such as the one in which Yonan had used his sword key. When they were in the midst of that he allowed them to stop and they ate the meat and drank from the gourds, but sparingly for they had not seen any source of water that day.

Kelsie was growing sleepy and longed to simply stretch out on the ground here and sleep away her weariness. Only Yonan made no sign of remaining where they were and her pride and stubborn desire to match him would not let her suggest a longer resting time.

Though she consulted the jewel now and then and was assured that they were following wherever that would lead them, she wanted more and more to drop it to this ground, let it be hidden by the tall grass, and return— Where?

In the day here Ben Blair seemed very far away in her mind, her whole life up to her coming through what Simon Tregarth had called a gate was more of a dream than her nightmare just past. She began to consider Yonan. He certainly was under no compulsion to travel so. Yet it was his knowledge which had saved them over and over again. He was not of the Valley by birth. That she knew. And he was even unlike most of the human kind who had gathered there. His hair was lighter and the eyes in his weather-browned face a startling blue. Who was Yonan? For the first time her mind wandered more from their present plight to ask a question. Dahaun apparently held him in repute having sent him after them for a guardian—or a guide. She had seen one of the other Tregarths—Kyllan—but there was nothing which appeared to make Yonan one of their out-breed stock. He usually companied with the huge axe weaponed warrior Urik. And there was that strange exchange which she had heard to suggest that he believed in reincarnation and had once been Tolar who had played some desperate game in this same land centuries ago.

"How far into this land have you been?" she suddenly asked.

He had paused to adjust the cord of his improvised shoulder bag and he did not look up as he answered:

"This land is new to me. Nor is it marked on any of the charts in the Valley."

"Yet you come with me—"

"I go with you," he returned, "since that is the duty laid upon me. When the witches out of Estcarp made contact with the Valley they bargained for guides. Nor did they understand that the influence of the Light flickers in many places and that there are powers upon powers which they have never heard of even within the records of Lormt."

Lormt! The place out of her half dream. Now she wanted straight answers. "What is Lormt?"

"A place in which ancient knowledge is stored. It was when Kemoc Tregarth went to Lormt that he learned of Escore—or at least that there was a country here to the east which had been forbidden to the Old Race who fled the adepts' war."

Now he arose and stood looking down at her. "What says your jewel? Which way?"

From her he had glanced at the wood about them. She had no desire to enter that darksome place of peril again but neither was there any sense in their remaining here in the open. So she dangled the gem hurriedly. It pointed again—more directly to the north Kelsie thought, though she was no forester or land dweller to guess aright at that signal.

The reed and illbane covering of their boots had shredded under travel and broken away so only bits of these remained. Also there were none of the herbs here and they could not renew that defense. Once more they entered the wood on the other side of the glade. There were no longer any faint traces of a trail and she noted that Yonan's pace had slowed. Now again he halted entirely, his head up as he sniffed the breeze, even as some animal advancing cautiously into unknown territory might test for some faint presence which was perilous to his kind.

There were still the arrow trees and the farkill so their advance was not straight because of these but took on a zigzag pattern. It was on one of their crawls to escape the arrow thorns that Kelsie set hand on what she thought was a round stone. Only to have it turn under her weight and grin evilly up at her—a skull! And, though there were differences in the wide ridges of bone above the eyes and the broadness of the whole, it approached that of a human. She uttered a little cry of disgust which brought Yonan's head around. But she had already noted two more of the grayish knobs a little before them and more—It was a pavement of skulls they had chanced upon!

Yonan shook his head when she asked what manner of creature had died here—here—and here—and there ahead—to form such a hideous track. But he kept to it even though she near refused to follow him. Then they came to the first of the monoliths.

The same grayish gleam of skull, of arrow tree, it stood out here in a half envelope of brush like a crooked giant finger pointing skyward—if there was indeed still an open sky above the ceiling of tangled tree branches.

The thing was taller than Yonan as he stood before it, and more bulky, but, though it was greened here and there with moss, it was easy to see that it had been purposely wrought into the form of a crouching image leaning forward a little—one massive arm raised and a great clawed hand or paw about to reach for some easily captured prey.

Kelsie sucked in her breath. She had seen many outré forms of life since she had so unwillingly begun this journey, but this was wholly malignant. The shoulders were bowed until it would appear that the creature it portrayed was humped. On those shoulders with a hardly visible neck perched a huge head, the bald cranium rising to a cone point. But it was the eyes which were the worst feature of that misshapen thing. They were as deep set as if they lay in pits. Yet they were not stone—or even inset gems—

She looked into them and gasped. Just like the hound that had appeared at the gate, these holes were filled with a yellowish flame. Stone and carven the monstrous thing might be. But—the eyes were alive! Was there some presence embedded in the stone—a prisoner without hope of freedom?

Without conscious thought she raised the Witch Jewel, not watching it as she did because she was entrapped by the fire in those stone-rimmed pits.

"No!" Yonan was upon her, his hand out to beat down the jewel. "No!"

She twisted in his hold, her fear grown a hundredfold. Only he had her arm so tightly pinned to her side that she could not break free to use what she had come to consider her only weapon.

"It is a watcher, let it not watch to any purpose," he added. Then thrust her away from him, so that meeting eye to eye with the thing was broken and she was free of what she now judged was indeed one of the more subtle dangers of this place.

Still holding onto her arm as if he feared she had not taken his warning to heart, Yonan pulled her along with him, their boots with the remnants of the illbane fastenings upon them slipping and sliding on the trail of skulls.

"It watched—was alive!"

"Not it but what watched through it," he countered. "If you had used the jewel you might have banished that watcher but you would have raised an alarm which—"

He stopped nearly in mid-word. There was another creature beside this noxious trail. It bore resemblance to the first but it was not graven stone—no, this was carved of wood. Some giant of a tree had been so used that the remnant of bark, now overgrown with leprous fungi, formed a skin, watched. There were the same pits of eyes—the same—after one fleeting glance she prevented her own sight with difficulty from meeting the eyes in the wood. They were also alive.

She pulled herself free of Yonan's grip and sped as well as she could down the skull road to avoid another meeting with that which so spied upon them. Now, as she went, she looked quickly from side to side to make sure there were no more of the watchers looming up before them.

No air stirred here under the trees, and there was a rising odor from the muck in which the skulls had been set which was putrid and sickening. There was a warmth here, too—not that protective one she knew when the jewel came to greater life, but rather a stifling sticky heat which eroded one's spirit as well as dragged at one's body.

However, the road led straight and she saw the ancient remains of trees which had been cut from their roots to clear a way for it. Here and there saplings had dared to reach up again, pushing aside the skulls which lay to grin at them. But they came across no more of the statues.

Not until they pushed through a last fence of brush and came to open country. The skull road had not stopped at their emergence into the open, though the bones here appeared to be more firmly planted.

"A road of the conquered," Yonan spoke for the first time since he had warned her in the wood. "It is very old that belief. To plant the heads of your enemies so that you tread ever upon them makes complete your victory." But Kelsie hardly heard him, she was looking ahead at the massive—thing—which had been erected there.

If she had believed the two she had seen in the wood were great and careful pieces of work, what could she call this?

For the road of skulls ran directly to a ponderous, outstretched belly of the thing squatting there—an artifact as large or nearly so as the ruin in which they had found themselves earlier. Both the hands were outspread and planted on the ground like giant pillars and those supported the huge form which was leaning forward as if to study whatever advanced toward it.

Twelve

There was a dark hole where the curve of its pendulous belly touched the ground. So regularly shaped it was that it could be a door— A door into what? Kelsie dared a quick glance up into the eye pits. But there was no hellish fire burning there, they were only dark caverns.

A harsh noise brought a small cry from her. Surely the thing before her was not alive, had not delivered such a hail. No, that had come from the winged things circling about its head. They were brilliantly scarlet even in this early eventide except for their bills and their feet—which were the black of the orifice opening at the end of the skull road.

They were stringing out, away from that perfect circle they had made about the head of the squatting thing, coming toward them. Yonan gave a cry in turn, one which perhaps was meant to hearten himself as well as any who heard. He hurled about his head the weighted cord he had used for hunting. But it was nothing for the pot that he would bring down now. The cord flew out, so quickly she hardly saw it go and wrapped itself about the long neck of one of the flyers, bearing the thing to the ground where it flopped and fought.

Yonan was ready for it with sword and a single sweep of blade whipped off the darting head. But he had to whirl then to beat off another flyer which swooped, dagger bill ready, to attack. Then that one, too, was left to flop on the ground headless but somehow still living.

Kelsie shouted and tossed up the jewel as a third sped down the sky aiming straight for her. She had little hope of beating it off—the thing was fully half her size, its wing spread was beyond her reckoning.

The jewel flickered with life and the bird sheered off. Kelsie's eyes following its flight fearfully saw something else. From the broad nose which covered near a third of the face of the demonic monster there puffed two small clouds of reddish smoke, thin and without any flame to feed them but they spread forward in the air, not diffusing as she thought that they would, rather to form a distinct cloud or blot. It was already under the film of twilight but that smoke—or breath—was still distinguishable.

The birds had attacked Yonan again, seeming to look upon him as the enemy they could bring down the easiest. He called to Kelsie, panting a little as he countered with sword against bill to keep his feet and break the attack.

"Do not let them circle! Break up that—!"

She swung the jewel, with no hope of contacting any of the flyers but noting that they fled the sparks which flew in the air from her only weapon. Then she was back to back with Yonan.

"Back to the woods?" she got out that question.

"Not with night coming," he told her. And she could understand the wisdom of that. They might escape the birds when they gained the shadows of the trees but they also would be girt about by a place of the Dark. At least in the open they could see their attackers.

Three of the birds had fallen to Yonan's sword but still the others attempted to build up a circle in the air above the two of them. And it was Yonan's constant thrusts which kept them from forming it completely.

Why they just did not fly higher and out of his reach Kelsie could not understand. But whatever plan governed them meant that they must travel close to the ground and fairly close to the two they would take.

She drew a deep breath and coughed, her throat rasped, her eyes burning. That breath from the monster was settling on them. She swung the chain of the jewel vigorously. That might keep off the birds but it had no effect upon the puff of crimson air. She coughed again, near strangled by the breath which she had been forced to inhale. There was a wretched burning, in her nose, her throat. Her eyes were beginning to water so she could hardly see. But still she strove to keep her feet and ward off this new peril—only it did not answer the jewel. Had she come to depend too much on that because so far it had not failed her? To everything there was a limit and here they two might have reached that.

For Yonan was also coughing hard. He stepped back and his shoulders were now against Kelsie's so she could feel the racking shudders which shook him. The birds cried out again even as they had done at their first coming—harsh squawks but ones which held a measure of triumph in them.

She felt Yonan slump and turned just in time to swing the jewel out to stop a vicious bill which was aimed for him as he crumpled to the ground. There was blood on that part of his face she could see below his helm and the helm itself had been knocked askew. The bird which had launched a fight attack on him was on the ground, its long legs holding well above it but its head drawn back for a finishing stab at the feebly moving man who was trying to regain his feet.

"No—circle—" he gasped.

But it was too late. Kelsie was coughing with such pain and depth that she felt her very lungs would be brought up by her choking. She could only hunch over Yonan holding above the two of them the Witch Jewel. And that one of the fearsome flock who had been about to impale her companion drew back and sidestepped from the run which would have carried it to that action.

Moisture from her tortured nose dripped down on Yonan and she saw it form beads of blood on his mail. Her throat was rasped so raw that nothing mattered now save that she could find some refuge from this poisoned cloud.

Through her tearing eyes she could see an open space

where the dancing red motes of the cloud made up the haze about them. On her knees, the gem in one hand, her other laced in Yonan's belt she strove to reach that promise of freedom.

She did not understand that she was being herded, not then. But she had a full moment of truth before the end came. The cloud lifted—she saw before her the black gap of an opening and only there was the promise of breath which had become a matter of life itself. One last effort— One effort and a momentary awakening to the danger— She had reached the ominous door in the monster's great belly and it was toward that she had crawled, dragging Yonan with her.

Kelsie strove to turn and the red haze settled. Coughing and tasting her own blood she fell forward into complete darkness in which she was lost.

Darkness again met her when she roused. For a moment she could not remember—and then the terror which had woven around her when she realized where they had been herded struck full force. She was not in that place of darkness where she had once been tossed, afraid and alone. No, she was truly awake and in a place of dark which was of this world. Her hands questing out on either side of her bruised and aching body were exploring over stone, rough and damp. Her fingers flinched away from a patch of slime.

She swallowed and her throat was sore burned by that last blast of the ruddy smoke. But this dark was so intense she was cold with another fear—that she was blind. She raised a hand feebly, for all her strength seemed drained and gone, rubbed across her closed eyes, opening them once more when she had done—upon thick dark.

Thick—for it seemed to have a quality of its own— smothering, holding her. Somehow she braced her hands on the floor and levered herself partway up, now depending upon her ears. There were no sounds—was hearing smothered and gone like her sight?

"Yonan!" There came no answer to her shout. Where-ever she was trapped, she was alone.

Now she felt for that which had lain on her breast—upon which she had come to depend. Her fingers closed upon a cold stone; it could be any pebble she might have taken up. The life and warmth she had sensed in it from the very first were gone. It was dead—

Dead? Perhaps this was death and she had come from life into an eternal dark.

It was only when that last fear began to crowd all control from her mind that Kelsie first became aware of something which was not sound but rather a vibration, growing ever stronger and sinking into her own body. It followed a regular series of beats yet there was no extra rhythm in it as had been in the bowl drums of the Thas. This was more like the measured thud of a heart—a heart so powerful that it could echo outside the body which held it.

The black gate in the belly of the monster—had she entered a thing with a life of its own? Her thoughts squirmed away from that—even in this country of strangeness and hallucinations such a thing could not be true.

She sat fully up in the dark and with her hands explored her whole body. The last remnants of the illbane wrappings were gone from her feet, but at her belt, snug in its own sheath was the long-bladed knife which was a part of all the clothing of a Valley dweller. She edged that out of its covering now, afraid of dropping it in this thick dark and losing her only weapon since it seemed that the power of the stone had deserted her.

Kelsie did not try to stand up. Keeping the knife ready she used her hand as a sweep before her. Always at the back of her mind was the fear that she was in truth blind and that her movements might well be under observation by those who had arranged her capture. Yet she could not remain huddled where she was awaiting some unknown attack.

There was the faint grating sound as her knife swept across the stone and that broke somehow the pattern of the beating which seemed to grow stronger the more she moved. Suddenly her hand stubbed against an obstruction of some sort and she quickly felt a barrier of stone as high as she could reach and as far as her arms on either side could stretch.

Now she did pull herself to her feet, running fingers along that wall as she arose. Where the floor had been cold, slime-dotted and forbidding, this wall differed in that there was a warmth to the stone the higher she reached—and it extended far above her head even when she stood on tiptoe.

The vibration which had reached her through the floor was more apparent here and she thought that somehow her own heart responded in beat to match that rhythm.

Now she began to move cautiously to her right. Feeling outward with the toe of one boot before she took any step with her weight upon it, running her fingers as a guide along the wall. The steady inpush of the dark around her made her doubly unsure of herself and she tested again and again her blind impression of what lay around her.

Then her hand slipped from the stone into open space—a door? She turned slowly with as much caution as she could summon. The flooring seemed secure enough. With knife she probed to her right and both heard and felt the touch of the blade to another obstruction. So—a door. Yet there was still no light to give her any help and she would have to travel anyway ahead with the same caution she had used before. Perhaps it would be better to explore the rest of the room before she attempted to use this other opening which might lead only to worse entrapment.

She sidled past that open space and once more encountered a wall under her touch. Now she began to count and was still counting when she discovered a sharp corner and changed her way to skirt a new wall. Three paces farther on was another opening and from that came a puff of air. Not the clean, lung cleansing breeze one could find in the outer world—this was moist and carried in it the stench of decay. Clearly *NOT* a way to follow.

Kelsie soon established that she had awakened in a room which had openings in three of its four walls, the third one much like the first one she had discovered. And it was between those two which she must choose now.

She returned to the first and ventured into something which her sense of touch said was a passage. Though she shrank from using her hands, as those patches of slime which she had found on the floor were here more numerous and often joined with one another when her fingers swept over them. She tried hard in her mind to build up a picture of where she was but without sight her imagination was limited and she was forced to understand that there was nothing she could do save that which she was doing, blindly venture into the dark tangle of this way.

As in that air which had puffed from the second passage she could smell corruption and once her fingers penetrated, before she could jerk them back, a mass of something clinging to the wall which squirted liquid, to burn her flesh as she hurriedly wiped her hand down her breeches, the evil smell so being carried with her.

The vibration was growing stronger and—she blinked, and blinked again. No she could not be mistaken, somewhere very far ahead there must be a source of light for the darkness was now not so complete. She hurried her pace and gave a small sigh of relief as that grayness overcame the blindness of the complete dark. Now she could see the walls and need not fear a second contact with the patches of dull black stuff which seemed to grow there as moss had done on the statue in the wood.

Yonan! At the far back of her mind all along there had rested the picture of the Valley warrior as she had seen him last, choking and sick from the fog. At least her explorations in the cell in which she had awakened had shown that he had not shared it. Where was he?

The gray light was tinged now with a faintly reddish gleam and she feared another encounter with that smoke which had undone them both, yet she could not yet turn away from light and seek the full dark again. The red became brighter. Her hands looked almost as if their blood within her veins had been drawn to the surface. It was warmer, much warmer also. And while the stench had grown worse there was no hint as yet of the choking gas if that was what the monster had exhaled.

Ten strides farther on and she came to another opening. Dropping to her knees she looked out into space where the red light glowed. She crept out on what proved to be a balcony or upper walk around a deep chamber, most of which lay beneath her, and there she froze, belly pressed to the stone, striving to see without being seen. For she was not alone.

There were at least a half dozen of them, she could not be sure because they came and went and only three remained steadily at their post which was on a similar balcony to the one she occupied but on the opposite wall of this deep opening.

Below was what amazed her the most. For there were humanlike figures there but here was also a vast tub or basin as big as a good-sized pool. It was filled not quite to the brim with a mass of what looked like thick red slime and it bubbled continuously as if aboil on some gigantic stove. As each of the bubbles on the surface broke they released a reddish mist which floated like a cloud, thinning to a kind of dribbling moisture which poured down again into the basined stuff.

Those who watched and came and went— Kelsie drew a deep breath and strove to make herself still smaller and less visible. That black-clad rider who had urged on the hound outside the stones—here was his like over and over again. The Sarn—! Feared as they were, not even the records of the Valley had had much to say about them or their deeds— save that they were wholly given to darkness and despair. They wore thigh-length cloaks over tight black covering which appeared modeled to their bodies, these cloaks having hoods as tight fitting with only apertures for eye holes. Their gloved hands moved in stiff jerky gestures as if it were by this method they conversed.

Kelsie's hand reached for the Witch Jewel. However, even as it had been on her first waking here, so was the gem cold and dead. The power she had come to lean upon had deserted her.

Twice one of the masked Sarn Riders had glanced upward

to where she crouched. So she flattened herself yet more but was not yet willing to withdraw from the chamber into the maze of dark passage behind her. There was a stirring below and she saw four other of the Riders come out of an opening to the side driving before them some captives. She had never seen the Thas in good light but there was no mistaking these creatures being hauled along by a rope knotted from one neck noose to the next, being pulled out into the dull red light of the ledge above that basin. They cowered and had to be dragged along. She was sure that over the ever hissing of the bursting bubbles she could hear thin, mewling, terror cries.

But the Thas were of the Dark—why had the Sarn taken prisoners from those on their own side? Or could it be that those of evil did not hang together by any desire save when such cooperation was demanded of them.

What she witnessed now shook her badly. Loosed from the first noose in that line the shaggy form of a Thas was thrust forward by the butt of a long pole held by two Riders. He—it—tottered for a frenzied second or two on the very edge of the ledge and then fell. This time it was easy to hear a grating scream as the creature was gone into the bowl of flame. The others in that line of sacrifice were tearing at the ropes about their own throats, pulling back on the ends the Sarn Riders held so firmly. As for their unfortunate fellow, he was swallowed up in the liquid fire and did not come to the surface once more.

Kelsie swallowed and swallowed again, again the raw sickness rising in her throat. If these Sarn Riders used one of their allies so—what death would they wish upon an enemy? She began to edge back inch by inch on the walkway which held her—though she had no wish to be hunted through the dark. There was another opening besides the one she had come through at the other end of the balcony and, after a moment of doubt and realization that to return to the cell where they had left her would avail her nothing, she chose to creep in that direction, keeping an eye on the Riders in the hopes of learning whether or not they watched her. However, they seemed completely intent on driving their captives to their doom one by one.

The girl gained that second doorway and crawled within it, finding that after a short distance it turned sharply to the right, seeming to run parallel to the chamber of the basin. Now it was dark. When she got well beyond the portal she got to her feet, for there were patches of growth along the walls which gave off a dull yellowish gleam, when her eyes adjusted to the dark. There were no side openings in those walls, and shortly she came to a flight of stairs leading down. Once more she hesitated and felt for the jewel. But it remained obstinately dead. She would have to rely on her own choices and powers. Where was Yonan? Kelsie was sickened by the thought that perhaps he had already been fed to the basin and that fiery thing which dwelt within it. Now that she was away from that actual chamber she was again aware of the steady beating vibration.

However, it was to go down or return and she knew that she had nothing to hope for in that direction. So she took the stairs step by step one hand feeling for any hold on the wall, for the patches of the yellow growth had in places swallowed a goodly portion of a step.

Kelsie counted again, trying to remember the position of the basin and guess whether this was carrying her below that or not. She had reached twenty when into her mind came that which for a moment wiped the memory of the Riders' hall from her.

"To the right—always the right—" She caught as a jog in the steps made her stumble and held on with both hands fearful for an instant at losing her step and plunging forward down this endless stair.

Yonan? Could that guiding have come from him? Somehow she could not tell. It was as if the mind voice which had sent it was hidden behind some distorting noise. Bait for a trap? She could not help but think of that. Yet if it *were* real and some other captive sought aid could she ignore it? There was always hope that the other would know more of this pile than she, and if she turned away she could be defeating the very purpose which had set her roving through the dark.

"Right—!"

The word faded and was gone. Kelsie took one step and the next with slow care, for here the yellow growth crossed the steps proving to be a jelly which gave forth a puff of foul decay. Then she had reached the level of another passage and sure enough it divided before her, right and left.

For the first time since she had awakened here she felt a faint warmth in the jewel and snatched it out. There was, in the very heart of it, a spark of light, far too small to aid her. But the very fact that it was able to project so much now heartened her. She turned right, one hand cupped tightly about the stone, following the direction given by that now silent voice. She made one attempt to use her own questing thought and then stopped that within almost the same instant. Among the terrors of this place there could also exist some method of picking up any mental communication and she did not have the use of the jewel strong enough to build up her call.

Again the way split and once more she tried the right-hand path. The eerie glow of the slime growths was augmented by a light from ahead—not the fearsome red of the basin chamber but more as if the flames of the leprous growths about her were increased a hundredfold. She was faced suddenly with a hole in the wall, but one which she must fall to her hands and knees to pass. Shrinking, sick from the odors which arose from the weird chamber before her instead of a passage.

There were growths here, also fungi perhaps, which had reached the height of small trees. Between them were smaller lumps of plants or mushroomlike things of different colors, as if in their misshapen bodies they aped flowers of the upper, clean world.

There was water also—or a liquid of some sort—which formed a small rivulet winding its way across the huge chamber. Its swollen looking waters were red and a haze arose above its length.

Through that she saw movement. Someone or something paced back and forth within the edge of the mist which spread out for a short space on either side of the stream.

Yonan! She dared not call his name, perhaps even think it. But she strode forward, trying to avoid contact with the smaller growth each of which when crushed added to the general foulness of the place.

Thirteen

There was no mail-protected fighting man across the mist-hung stream—though that other went clad in gray instead of in black as a Sarn Rider. There were rents in that long robe and hair hung in a tangle across the pacer's shoulders. Though she had lost the iron-bound neatness and sobriety of her garments there was no trouble in recognizing—Wittle!

The witch came to a stop as Kelsie approached the riverlet and now she stood with both hands cupping her own jewel with such intensity as to leave her knuckles hard knobs in her pallid skin.

"So it is you—" there was no trace of welcome in her voice and there was certainly no expression of it on her angular features.

"How did you come here?" Kelsie returned. Was Wittle able to use her jewel—if so how did she end in this noisome place of the Dark Force.

"There was a trail—it proved false." The witch replied shortly. "And how came you?"

"We were taken, outside." She believed that the door in the monster's belly had led her here. "Does your jewel aid you now?"

There was a flush up Wittle's spare cheeks which was not a reflection from the blood-red stream. For a space of two breaths Kelsie thought she was not going to answer. Then she said:

"Its power is greatly diminished but it is not dead. And what of the one you so falsely wear, outworlder?"

"It is still alive." Kelsie was sure of that spark of warmth which had arisen after she had left the cavern of the basin. "I cannot call it though."

"Well you cannot!" snapped Wittle. "Would you have these creatures of the Dark realize what they have taken? Come hither and join me, perhaps the gems, stone to stone, will give us true sight in spite of what lies around."

Kelsie had no intention of wading that steaming stream. She turned and walked along it to see if it narrowed enough for her to essay a leap to the other side. Within short space of time it did—though the rank growth on the other bank suggested no fair landing. But what Wittle had half promised was worth the try.

She drew back again and then approached the stream at a run vaulting over it and landing in the mass of fungous material which burst and broke under her weight, smearing her with a stench borne by viscid splotches. She kept herself from trying to brush the stuff from her for fear of some poison—for she could not believe that such a loathsome medley of stinking smears would not also prove poisonous. Wittle awaited her but bore back a step or two as the fetid smells grew worse at every move Kelsie made.

She pointed to a bare space where she had paced. There was a patch of loose gravel there and Kelsie gingerly scooped up some of that to brush the worst of the stuff from her body.

"The jewel!" Wittle did not leave her much time to try to cleanse herself. She advanced, her own stone lying across both of her palms, and Kelsie obediently did the same with the gem on her own neck chain. They touched and immediately there was a small flare and thereafter a core of light in each of them.

"So—they can be fed!" Wittle was exultant. "Let us see."

She settled down on the bare gravel, still careful that her torn robe did not touch Kelsie's beslobbered garments. With one hand still on her stone she laid it down and motioned for Kelsie to do likewise. The girl hesitated.

"And if we awake the Dark?" Kelsie asked. "You, yourself, have said that this could be so—"

"You would wait here for them to come? What profit for us in that? Already they know that they have a Witch of Estcarp." She drew herself up proudly. "They will expect no more than that I try my strength against theirs. That it be doubled now—well, that may be enough to penetrate some of their barriers."

Slowly Kelsie placed her own jewel beside that other one, taking care to have it touch Wittle's. The result was like a small fire, for the heart flame in each shot upward for an eye dazzling space and then died down into a steady double glow.

"The way out—" Wittle leaned forward her tongue caressing her lower lips as if she had just drunk deeply of some restoring drink.

But Kelsie was as quick with her own demand. "Yonan!"

The witch snarled and put out her hand as if to snatch away her jewel, but she did not quite break the connection between them.

"The way out!" She put her face forward, so close to Kelsie's that a small fleck of spittle hit the girl's cheek. "The man is useless—we must be on our way."

"Yonan," Kelsie repeated with stubborn determination. If she had to choose between traveling companions she already was certain which one she would take.

It would appear that Wittle did not feel strongly enough to gainsay her now for as Kelsie centered her gaze on the two glowing stones and built up in her mind her picture of Yonan as she had last seen him, the witch did not protest again. Though if she added her own focusing power to that search Kelsie had no way of telling.

There was a curdling of the light about the two stones. In that they themselves disappeared but there came a surface flat and shining like a mirror and on that formed a shadow which grew into a distinct picture. There was thick darkness there but a small gleam of light showed a hand gripping a sword hilt. Between fingers that light found its way and Kelsie knew or guessed that Yonan's scrap of the Quan iron was still alive. Black shadow moved against shadow and she believed, though the sighting was so bad, that the Valley warrior was moving through the same lightless kind of passage which she had dared upon her awakening here.

She leaned across and fairly hissed at the witch:

"Call! With me call if you ever wish my aid again!"

"Yonan!" she shaped the word in her own mind and suddenly felt an inflow of aid. She had managed to enlist Wittle after all. "Yonan!"

She saw that dark shadow halt and the fingers slip from the hilt to the blade beneath. The Quan took on a deeper gleam and the shadow which surely was Yonan swung to the right. Kelsie reached for the arm of the witch and felt her finger bite deeply into the other's spare flesh.

"Call!"

"Yonan," at each repetition of that name, aided by, she was sure, the picture she continued to hold in her mind, that shadow moved now more swiftly as if on the track of something which brushed the risks of chance from its passage.

There was light in the dark, dim and hard to see—the girl thought of the glimmer of the fungi along the walls. She saw the man with the sword. They had left him his mail along with his weapon. Perhaps it was the latter their captors had feared, not for its point (though she knew he had made good play with that) but for the talisman bound into its hilt. Just as they had not taken her jewel.

"Yonan!"

There came a faint answer. "I come!"

"Fool!" If Wittle had aided in that first call she was no longer doing so now. "What need have we for him? These," she touched her own jewel lightly, "are enough to win us out."

"I call one who is one of us—" Kelsie began, her temper rising in that inner heat which might lead to such recklessness as that which had brought her into this perilous land in the beginning. "He—"

"Is a man!" The witch interrupted her. "What power has he beside the power of fighting arm? We need no weapon—"

"Except these," Kelsie reminded her, pointing to the two stones between them.

Wittle grimaced. "The power is overlaid by this about us. We shall have to use it to the best of our ability to call. Were you one of the sisters—" her voice died away but there was still in her eyes the animosity which Kelsie had always seen there.

"I am not!" Kelsie was quick to deny. She did not know why the jewel had come alive in her hands but she refused to believe that some part of her was akin to this thin, bitter woman.

"Where are we?" she asked.

Wittle pursed her lips as if she doubted the need for Kelsie's question. Then she answered:

"This is a place of the Sarn Riders. Of them we know but little—"

"And none of it good," Kelsie finished when she hesitated. "Who are they, then?"

"They serve some great Dark One. Who they are and why they serve . . ." she shrugged. "Both Light and Dark draw together strange partners. In Estcarp we would know. Here," she made a small gesture with the hand which hovered over the jewel, "I cannot say. Those in the Valley hold by only one of the true adepts. There may be more of those left. Not all were eaten up by their enemies or withdrew into other worlds." For the first time she seemed to be under the urge to talk. Kelsie was very content to let her. The more she could learn the better, even though much of what Wittle said could be guesses only.

"These adepts—" she encouraged.

"They are the ones who would rule all. Some withdrew

and were neither of the Light nor the Dark but followed paths of their own. Others struggled for power and there were wars, ah, such wars! Even the earth was wrung by the strengths they called upon. For the tissue of life itself can be changed if the will is great enough."

Kelsie thought of the stories she had heard in the Valley. "Did not those sisters of yours reach such powers? Did they not move mountains with their words of command, so that the enemy could not come upon them?"

"And so they died," replied the witch somberly. "For the power we called upon then burnt out many of the sister-hood. Thus—it is thus we must find that which will recharge our jewels to a greater holding than they have ever known."

"And this greater power, do you think that you will find it here?"

"It was pulling us—for like is pulled to like, and with the stones charged with the same energy we shall be led to the source of it. No, fool, it does not lie hereabout or none of this," again she made that small one-handed gesture, "would exist. Here," she reached behind her and pulled forward a travel-stained pack, much like the one Kelsie had lost in the burrow of the Thas. "Eat and drink—"

As if those two words had been a signal both her dry throat and her empty stomach made themselves known. The girl pulled out a metal flask and allowed herself a few sips of insipid and musty tasting water. This was followed by crumbs of a half-eaten round of journey bread. But the stench of the rank growth about her took much of her need for food. That smell rendered nauseating all she ate or drank.

Wittle leaned forward once again and was peering intently into the halo of dim light which circled about the two stones, springing from their point of touch. She began to intone in a voice hardly above a whisper, using her forefinger to sign in the air. Though there was no blue-lined answer to her now.

Kelsie crowded forward to see any picture which the

stones might produce. But what she did perceive was instead lines of what might have been an unknown script. And she worried about the summoning of such in the very heart of one of the enemy strongholds.

Wittle was still repeating queer singsong uttered words in a murmur when Kelsie turned her head sharply and strove to look over her shoulder. The sense of being watched had come suddenly but it was so strong she was not surprised to see a figure dimmed by the fog of the red stream coming forward.

She had her knife and it was ready in her hand. At her hissed warning Wittle did not even look up or break her concentration upon the stones. But a moment later Kelsie was on her feet, moving through the haze, jerking from the ground the gem as she went to call to that shadow figure.

"Yonan! Here!"

Her call was near drowned out by a screech from Wittle as the stone against stone formation was broken. The witch sprang at Kelsie, clawing for the chain swinging from her hand. So that the girl had to turn and beat off her attack and did not see Yonan make the same spring which had brought her earlier to this sliver of ground free from the noisome vegetation.

"The stone—give it to me!" Wittle cried. "Almost I learned—stupid wench. Almost I had touched upon what rules here!"

"But glad that you did not!" It was Yonan who answered that. There was a smear of dried blood, bits of it flaking off as he spoke, down the side of his face. He had one arm across his chest, the hand thrust into his sword belt and there were pain lines about his mouth. But he was gripping his sword by the blade close to the hilt and the Quan iron was fully revealed.

"This is Nexus—" he added as he came closer.

To Kelsie the word meant nothing and she thought that Wittle was similarly ignorant until suddenly a shadow crossed the witch's sharp features.

"That is legend—" she said in that same sour voice she had always used when she spoke to Yonan.

"Much in Escore is legend come to truth," he said. "How did you get here—did you not see the Fooger Beast—?"

"I slept for I was wearied; I awakened here," the witch returned. "The Fooger—!" It was as if she had bitten on something harsh and stinging.

"The Fooger. We are within it, Witch. And I do not think that any power of yours is going to get us out."

She pointed to the gem still swinging from Kelsie's hand. "There are two of these and," she gestured at his sword, "and what you carry."

"These against that which shaped the Fooger—" His lips quirked at the edges into something which was certainly not a smile but suggested derision.

"Small stones to bring down the enemy full armed and with weapons which we may not have known before. How come you here, Lady?" He swung so sharply to Kelsie that she stammered over the first word of her answer. But she told as swiftly as she could of her journey down the dark passages and her final emergence guided by the witch to this place.

His frown grew. "Thus I was brought also—by your calling on me. Have you thought that perhaps that which holds us wanted us together so that it might wait and see what we should do then, what power we can summon to break us out?"

Kelsie accepted the logical reasoning of that but Wittle shook her head vigorously. "Such as you envision, warrior, would not wish even the smallest of Light weapons to be used within its hold. Balanced always is the power and if that balance shifts but a trifle, the merest finger's breadth or less, then all within its range are affected. Why do you think they left us these?" she waved her jewel in Yonan's face. "Because they cannot handle what might be provoked into life should they meddle with them. Yes, it is true that they may have brought us together for some purpose of their own but also it may be as a test—to see if we dare to stand up to their might.''

"You speak of 'they,'" Yonan said. "Who are these then? Sarn Riders and Thas? Their like we know. But the Fooger—''

"Is perhaps lying dead!" snapped Wittle. "What is death but a gate and we of the mysteries know many gates. Was not the adept Hilarion summoned back through the one he himself had opened when the Tregarth traitoress went a-meddling? So I speak of 'they' and you would know who and what they may be? Think upon your darkest nightmare and then count that light against what comes from the Dark, warrior.''

"If they would test us, why bring us together?" he said musingly as if he asked that question of himself and not of Wittle. But Kelsie thought she could answer that.

She had settled down again on the sweep of clean gravel and was slipping the jewel from one hand to another.

"They would see what we can do when we try to defend ourselves—the three of us together—''

Wittle favored her with a grimace. "Have I not already said it? And have we not already given them a showing of banner in that we *HAVE* come together?''

Yonan stood looking about the cavern. It was perhaps larger than the one which held the basin of fire, but the most of it was choked by the growth. And the constant stench of that made Kelsie nauseous so that she was like to lose the small mouthfuls she had taken. It was Yonan who moved first. Without a word to Wittle he used the Point of his ensorceled weapon and drew about the three of them a five-pointed star, digging deep in the sand and gravel to keep the line intact. Wittle watched him and for the first time Kelsie saw a shade of astonishment on the witch's face.

"What would you do?" she demanded. He neither answered nor looked to her but out of his belt pouch he took a mass wrapped in a withered leaf. Kelsie caught the unforgettable aroma of illbane. At each point of the star he faced outward and, spearing a bit of the crushed herb on his sword point, he planted it in the ground.

"Fool!" Wittle came to life and moved as if to erase the marking nearest her. He swung around and in a quick movement slashed downward before her the sword as if so locking her in.

"They will come," she screeched at him, both her hands cupping her jewel. "To set up a place of power within their own holding—you are a madman."

"I am one," he returned, "who wants to see his opponent. Fighting blind here will avail us nothing. Do you," now he spoke directly to Kelsie, "take your jewel and," he turned a fraction toward Wittle, "you know the signs—use them and let her follow. We are now locked within this hold, better that we learn what will come of us—"

For a long moment Kelsie thought Wittle would refuse. Then stiffly as if each gesture she made was forced out of her, she knelt and reached out one long stick-thin arm so that she might use the point of her jewel to draw in the slipping ground a line here, a circle there—and more intricate symbol somewhere else. When she had done in the first of the points Yonan gestured to Kelsie so that the girl squatted on her heels and tried to copy the signs—though she doubted much her ability to match them, so loose was the soil. Around the inner part of the star the two of them crept, Kelsie duplicating as best she could all that Wittle did.

She had more than half expected that the witch would utterly defy Yonan's orders, yet she tamely obeyed him. Perhaps within her she thought that what they did might establish—for a space—an island of safety.

Only it was not meant to work that way. For when she had done and arose, Kelsie behind her, she favored Yonan with a display of yellowish teeth which surely was no smile.

"SO—the bait awaits, warrior. What do you expect to bring into being by defying the balance here?"

"What you wish to see as well as I," he replied. "I do not fight blind when there is a chance of seeing openly."

"You shall see," she cackled. "Oh, yes, you shall see!"

Kelsie swung about where she stood and began carefully to examine the vegetation on each side, turning slowly. So grotesque was that growth and in such tangle anything might be creeping upon them now unseen until it reached the very edge of the open space. That they were now bait she firmly believed.

But as the minutes passed, her heart beat slowly. She could see nothing moving and the growth remained the same. Nor did anything come out of the river. Wittle spoke first.

"They know how helpless we are," she said grimly, "why trouble themselves with us?"

"Balance," Yonan said firmly. "Balance. In the heart of their own holding there is this." With his sword he pointed to the star about them. It seemed to Kelsie that she could smell the fragrant freshness of the illbane combating the stench of the growth.

A tendril of haze snaked out from that murk which clothed the stream. It was almost like the weighted line Yonan had used to bring down the birds in his hunting, but this was aimed at them. It curled like the lash of a whip through the air. But when it reached the star it snapped back.

Wittle again made that harsh sound which was her laughter. "Do you think that is all they have to send against us?" she demanded.

Yonan did not answer. He had stooped and picked up one of the small stones which studded the sand at his feet. Now he blew upon it and then spat, rubbing the moisture into it with his thumb. Having done so he rubbed the stone three times against the Quad iron of his sword hilt and called upon a name Kelsie had heard him summon before.

"Ninutra!"

Out toward the questing tongue of haze he hurled the stone. It passed through that arm of mist and that lifted for a moment so that Kelsie saw the stone fall into the red river. The liquid there roiled, churned, droplets arose to sprinkle the vegetation which straightway fell into a black liquid rot. And the mist snapped back toward its source.

"Child's play!" Wittle said. "And who is Ninutra? Some Old One long since gone?"

"If she has gone," he replied, "then she has left certain strengths behind her. I serve a Lady who is her chosen voice in the here and now. And—"

"Look!" Kelsie interrupted him.

From out of the river where the stone had fallen there arose something which chilled and sickened her. Perhaps once it had had life—it must have had—but this was the worst of death's decay incarnate. Half-skeleton, half-boiled and seared flesh, it was tossed ashore as if the river itself had so sent one of its slaves to dispute with them. Was it a man—or had it been a man? Kelsie wanted to close her eyes, to refuse to look upon it but she could not.

Slowly, clumsily it got to its feet and for the first time turned the blob of its head in their direction. Kelsie cried out. Those swollen, bloated features were ones she knew— Yonan's!

She heard him whisper from beside her. "Urik—NO!" While Wittle seized upon her jewel and cried out "Make-ease!"

The half-eaten away features of the thing writhed and changed—now the girl saw Dahaun wasted and blasted, and after her Simon Tregarth. While from her companions, she heard other names given to that nightmare.

It tottered on legs which were bare bone, heading for the star. Kelsie gripped the jewel and in her mind refused any belief—this could not be true. It was not true! Even as the thing became Yonan once more she cried out:

"No—it is not true!"

Yonan—that was no longer Yonan, nor Dahaun, nor the eldest of the Tregarths. It was her own blasted face which crowned the shambling figure.

Fourteen

It wavered to and fro on its bony feet as it continued to advance and Kelsie cowered back, though Wittle's hand shot out and caught at her before she stepped outside the star.

"Illusion!" croaked the witch, though Kelsie saw her straight mouth twitch as if she barely stifled some cry of her own. "They play with illusion!" She held out her hand, pointing her gem toward the thing from the rivulet.

There was no bright sword thrust of power as there had been on other occasions, only a small diffusion of a bluish haze clinging around the stone itself. And still the horror came ahead. Yonan raised his sword to ready. But the thing had reached the edge of the star and shifted from one foot to another as if it were faced by an impassable barrier.

"Ah—" the sound came from Wittle like a long drawn out sigh of relief. "By so much the old knowledge holds— by so much!"

The shambling figure turned first right and then left as if trying for a free path to reach its prey. It seemed to Kelsie that it grew more solid and real every moment. It was still her own face that it half wore, though she believed now that it showed another countenance to each of the two with her. There was a wavering, the thing swayed back and forth and then plunged forward as if some giant hand aimed at its back had sent it so to confront them. It fell across one of the points of the star and there was a blast of light which left Kelsie blinded, then with blurred sight.

Where the figure had fallen there was a stinking mass of stuff which still moved feebly as if the force which had given it pseudo life still urged it on. Then it crumpled away to black ash. But it had been the key to unlock the fort Yonan had erected and Kelsie felt the chill of the utter dark through which she had once passed sweep in over that break point. Though she could see nothing, that cold clung to her, wrapping her in and she felt a viscid stuff netting her prisoner. Wittle's arm with the hand which held her jewel beat at the air and Yonan slammed out with his sword hilt, the blade gripped with his fingers. All to no purpose.

Kelsie was motionless. That invisible web had her entirely in its power now, she could not even move a finger across the surface of her own jewel. She saw Wittle's arm fall to her side as if struck down by some heavy blow, Yonan's reversed sword play fail. They were all caught by what had won through the boundaries of the star. Then, against her will and by no action of her own, the hand which held the chain of her jewel began to quiver and shake. However, her fingers locked on the links did not move. Back and forth, more and more wildly shook her hand, the gem swung but it did not fall, nor did it part company with her flesh. She had a sudden mind picture of the jewel flying out to land in the red rivulet and being overwhelmed, that if she would save her life this is what must happen. Then over that slid another picture, the young witch who had died on the hillside, her lips shaping her own forbidden name as she gave that to Kelsie. With her was another head also, that of the wildcat, its lips drawn back in a full snarl, daring McAdams, ready to spend its life for its kits and freedom.

Around and around whirled her arm and the pain of those wild swings which pulled at her muscles grew more intense. There was also a twisting now, a pulling. And still the chain clung to her as if it were a part of her own flesh and nothing would take it from her unless the enemy, whoever or whatever that might be, would scrape that from her bones. Twice she cried out against sudden shocks of pain, in spite of her promise to herself that she could and would endure.

She could see both Wittle and Yonan. They stood statue stiff and neither of them appeared under attack. Did what assailed them believe that she was the weakest of their company, the only most likely to give way? Somewhere under the fear which had held her since that creature had come out of the mist anger stirred. That emotion grew as the assault upon her doubled in its fury.

Deliberately now she summoned up the picture of the young witch who had died. She could not call upon Wittle—perhaps she was held now against a similar attack—but she was trained, one with her stone as Kelsie did not feel herself to be. As the cat had faced McAdams so did she snarl and stand trying to wrest from that other power the control over her own body.

She had a sense of anger and frustration—not her own but coming from somewhere beyond. Then she was struck a sudden buffet between her shoulders, driving her to her knees, and was enveloped in that sharp stench which was the mark of the evil.

Something cried out in a high squalling voice and now came a blow on the back of her head, sending her flat with a weight on her back. Gravel gritted against her cheek and her body rocked under blows. Her arm was seized and drawn backward at a painful angle. Once more her wrist snapped to and fro under vigorous shaking. The chain remained as much a part of her as the fingers curved about the links. She tried to throw off the weight upon her and managed to shift her face around to see one of those which bestrode her— shaggy, rootlike covering—Thas.

The servant of the Sarns grabbed at her hand. She felt the sharp pain of teeth in her flesh and then there was a convulsive jerking to the body perched on hers and the Thas rolled off to lie beside her, its rootlike fingers, its thin arms, threading wildly in the air. She caught a glimpse of red eyes in the ill-fashioned face and then those eyes clouded. The limbs fell to the gravel limply and there was no more struggle out of it.

Yonan—had he won to freedom and used his sword? Wittle she could see, still standing, still staring not at the struggle on the ground at her very feet, but at the haze which masked the rivulet as if she expected some further attack out of that.

Kelsie tried to draw up one foot, get to her knees. The cold shell still held a part of her but the attack of the Thas appeared to have broken through it and now it was as if pieces of net tore and fell away.

She dragged her arm around and saw the tooth marks on her wrist slowly welling with blood which striped both the chain and the stone it supported. Her body ached from the attack but slowly she won to her knees, her hurt wrist nursed against her body.

Yonan stood even as Wittle faced outward. But she could see his features, not set as those of the witch, but his eyes striving to catch hers. His mouth open as if he shouted some war cry she could not hear.

On impulse she reached out with the hand dripping blood and set it to his mail-clad thigh which was nearest her. A shudder ran through his body and he turned his head fully to look at her. A moment later he had stooped to support her, draw her up to her feet leaning against him, the dead Thas kicked aside that he might come closer. If Wittle was still bound it was plain that he had been freed.

He reached out to take her bitten arm and then his fingers snapped back as if they had been beaten off. Whatever had kept chain and stone with her during that attack was still in force. Now Yonan brought his sword around, cautiously advancing the hilt so that it was in touching distance of that invincible chain.

The Quan iron slid easily through and over, caught at a loop of the chain, drawing that away from the wound which was bleeding steadily.

Kelsie felt her other arm and hand tingle as if recovering from some paralyzing force. She put out her finger and touched the chain. At her touch they loosened and she was able to take jewel and chain into her other hand.

She sat at last, the throbbing in her wrist not unlike that beat of the vibration around them, her injured wrist resting on her knee where Yonan had placed it after binding it with a strip of her own shirt and some of the dust of the illbane he had managed to shake out of his bag. Wittle had blinked and then turned her head to look at the two of them, as if just awaking from a dream. Yonan had booted the body of the Thas out of the star but, though he redrew it with sword point, he had not enough of the herbs left for its guarding points.

"You have not won—" Wittle broke the silence which had held them all from the moment of the Thas attack. "This was merely a feint to learn what powers we held."

And it picked me, Kelsie thought, though she did not speak her guess aloud, as the weakest point in our defenses. Yonan might have guessed her belief for he said:

"They sent the Thas. They would not have used such force if they had believed they could take us by will and power alone. They—"

Kelsie slipped the chain of the jewel about her neck again and it rested on her breast just above where she cradled her bitten wrist against her body. "Who are *they*?" As she had tried to learn earlier from Wittle so she asked him now.

"Old ones—perhaps even an adept tied somehow to this land. Only he caught, with his force, something which he can neither digest nor subdue." Yonan was again at the star redrawing the lines. "In the heart of his own place he has . . . us!"

Wittle turned her head. Her face was expressionless but her eyes glittered. When she spoke it was directly to Kelsie, ignoring the warrior:

"What have you, outlander, which stands so against the Dark? What is the power that you control?"

Kelsie shook her head. "No power that I know of. They will be back?" Once she had stood up to the battle, a second one she was not sure she could face.

"As he said," Wittle pointed with her chin to where Yonan stood, feet slightly apart as if about to engage in combat, all his attention now for the haze about the stream, "we are within territory where the lord here, whoever or whatever he may be, would destroy us—or have us forth. Warrior!" she raised her grating voice a fraction. "Look to your sword. We have yet to face the worst they can send. What does one do to a piece of grit within one's boot—one shakes it out. It may well be that he or it—or she—cannot use full strength here lest the defenses of this place be damaged. Therefore—it will shake us forth—"

As if her words had been the recital of a spell there came a sudden change to that ribbon of fog about the river. It split and peeled away on either side revealing the narrow part of that shore, which Kelsie had earlier leaped to come here, and held so—clearly an invitation to leave.

Leave so that they could be easily hunted down in some one of the passageways which ran from this cavern? Kelsie's wrist throbbed and her other hand cupped over the jewel could have held only dull stone for all its response to that invitation.

Slowly Yonan worked his way out to the place where the noisome thing from the stream had essayed its attack. He carefully skirted the shriveled mass on the sand and stood now at the very edge of the rivulet. Reaching forward he put out the hilt of his sword toward the nearest clump of the fungilike growth.

It moved, actually pulling away from the Quan iron. Wittle, as if not to be left behind, had swung out her jewel and the misty emanation from that, nebulous as it was, had the same effect on another of the bulbous plants. Under Kelsie's hand her own stone moved and grew a little warmer.

"Can you foresee?" Yonan rounded on the witch. "Is that gem of yours a compass for our going?"

She shrugged. "Who knows. But if we remain here we shall never know, shall we?"

Kelsie bit her lip. To go out of this small haven of safety

broken though it was now—she could not raise a voice to say yes. The pain in her wrist had spread up her arm, was slowly fighting a way into the rest of her body. She was not even sure she could get once more to her feet and go now. Yet the witch, as if to show the strength of her own charm and power, had passed Yonan, taking the lead and swinging the stone from side to side as she went until she kilted up the stained skirt of her robe and sprung across the stream. Yonan turned to Kelsie holding out his free hand and once more pulling her up beside him.

"She is right,"he said, "To remain here self chained and wait for what more they can send against us—that is folly."

She allowed him to lead her to the stream bank, wanting to close her eyes lest some new horror arise from there to take them as they crossed. But cross they did and without any interference from what dwelt here. But to get out—that was a different matter and in her innermost mind Kelsie never believed they could or would make it. They would wander through the warren of passages until hunger and thirst weakened them to be easy for the taking, or some other servants of the Dark would run them down. She remembered very well the hounds of the Sarn and those grim Riders themselves.

Wittle stalked ahead and was entering one of the passage openings before they had caught up with her. The pain which had earlier been like fire in her veins now left Kelsie's wrist and arm limp and numb. She staggered now and then but Yonan's hand was always ready to support her.

Back in the passage it was dark, only the scattered patches of growth gave them thin light and those grew further and further apart as they passed. Kelsie listened as she went, sure that she would hear soon sounds of pursuit, yet those did not come. Perhaps they were in some manner being herded toward a place where they would be easier to handle. Why Wittle moved so unceasingly, seeming to find choice between passages so easy to make, the witch did not explain.

Now there was light ahead—not a red glare, nor the

sickly glimmers thrown off by a multitude of fungous vegetation—rather a gray gleam rounded a corner and was gone. Yonan led Kelsie after and they came out suddenly into an opening which drew a cry from Kelsie as she pulled backward two or three steps which might have ended in a ghastly fall.

The three of them were crowded on a space which could hardly support them. And they were high in the air above red stone. Kelsie held with her good hand to the edge of the door from which they had just emerged. But Yonan edged forward to look down into the space which surrounded them.

In a moment he was back. Wittle had seemed to drop once more into one of her possessed times when nothing about her could matter.

"We are on the monster's head," the warrior reported. "We must climb down."

Kelsie nursed her numb hand and arm and remembered only too well how the monstrous carving or building had towered above the skull road they had followed. She had no hope of daring to descend the outer surface of that. No wonder they had passed so unchallenged through the last ways. She did not doubt that the enemy knew exactly where they were and had a good method of handling them in this exposed position. Why, an eruption of Thas from the mouth where she now rested could send them out into space. To say nothing of what the Sarn Riders could do with their fiery bolts.

"There is no way down," she said dully.

He was standing over her again and now he pulled her to her feet with less gentleness than he had used before.

"There is a way!" His voice was an imperative as if he had shouted in her ear.

"Look!" he pointed out a moment later.

There was an overhang beneath where they stood and the flare-out of a rounded ledge. All was pitted by time's erosion with holes for fingers and feet. Were it not for her wrist pulsating with dull pain she conceded she might be able to climb down. But one handed she could not begin to try. However, it seemed that Yonan had taken that also into consideration.

He was working at the clasp of his sword belt and had that free before she could protest. Now he reached for her again.

"Your belt!" he demanded. One handedly she tried to obey, only to have him push aside her hand and open the clasp himself. Then he buckled two ends together, testing them over his bent knee. He set together the end of her own belt in a sling which he motioned her to put over her good shoulder and drew her to the lip of the drop.

"Down!"

Because she inwardly shrank from that action she set her teeth and made herself crawl over, dangling in a sickening fashion out into space, refusing to look at anything but the pitted stone before her until her boots did thud home on the bubble of the cheek of that hideous visage and she looked perforce into one of the eye holes. She flinched away and pulled herself as far from that as she could get. For in its depth either memory played her false or she had seen the reflection of the flames which had danced in the bowl of that chamber of death she had spied upon.

Yonan had said nothing to Wittle but apparently the witch had decided on her own that escape was possible and she came down from one handhold to the next. However, Yonan won there before her and then busied with Kelsie lowering her farther—to the thing's puffy shoulder.

She was wet with sweat when a last swing brought her to the ground after a time she had no desire to remember. Twice she had knocked the elbow of her wounded hand and the pain of that nearly made her sick so that it had been hard to even think what she was about until she made a last descent from the monster's folded knee and felt dry earth under her weak and shaking legs. Then Yonan was beside her and she saw through eyes dimmed with tears of pain the back of the witch who was striding away from them as if she no longer chose to be one of their company.

Yonan got Kelsie to her own feet and steered her in the direction of the witch, keeping a close hand on the belt which still hung from her shoulder. Every moment when she could think at all beyond the pain of her arm Kelsie expected to hear from behind the hoarse bellowing of a hound, perhaps the shout of a Sarn Rider urging on a hunt. But there was nothing.

She turned to the warrior who was half supporting her. "They will not let us go—" she got out that protest.

"Have they in truth?" he returned. "They seek what that one," he nodded to the witch now well ahead of them, "came here to find. Why not give her an illusion of freedom and let her lead them to what they would have also. Do you think that they have put aside all interest in why we roam where those of the Light have not ventured much before?"

"Then—you believe that it was all play with us?" she faltered. Three mice and a sleepy-eyed cat that let its prey run a little and then brought down a paw to end the game.

"Some of it was testing, I think. But I also believe that had they not wished it we would never have come alive out of that place."

She tried to push aside his grim reply but the logic of it was too sound. They were mice, allowed to run. And there were those or *THAT* which would watch them well from now on.

However, if Yonan believed in what he said he acted as if their escape had been a true one, keeping a good pace and helping Kelsie to equal it. She purposely did not look back, for, in her mind, was a picture of the squatting monster rising leisurely and setting out in their wake ready to bring stamping foot or clutching hand upon them when and if it wished.

They had come to a tangle of growth—not the fleshy fungi of the inner ways but rather rank stuff with good-sized thorns, and it seemed to be so matted and grown together there was no way to get through it.

Only Wittle still in advance swung out her jewel which flashed as it never had in the inner ways and sparks from it fell into the mass from which arose small twists of smoke and a backaway shriveling of the growing stuff.

If the witch believed also that they were allowed to run free just to bring their search to an end, she showed no sign of that, nor did she do anything to cover her trail. But the brush flaked swiftly into ash and parted before her and the other two followed where she led. Kelsie wondered how much longer she could keep her feet to stumble on. The pain had risen to her shoulder and was now moving over across her breast so that she could hardly draw a full breath. She wanted nothing so much as to lie down, close her eyes, and fall into a black nothingness.

Nor was she aware when the brush about them ceased to be an entwined matting of thorns and became fresh and well growing bushes, some with flowers enough to give forth scent. Save that she was free at last of the stench of the burrows. Kelsie was indifferent to everything but the claims of her own hurt body and she roused only when Yonan's grip, which had grown more and more compelling, lightened and she was lowered to the ground.

From somewhere came the sound of running water— water or fire? She strove to struggle up again to make sure she was not back in the cavern. Wittle, bending over her, pushed her back and the other's touch on her body brought with it such a thrust of pain that she dropped back into darkness at last.

There was a time when a fire did burn not too far away. And she was aware that the belt held now not her hurt arm but her good one. There was a punishing weight on her hurt arm and shoulder, so that she cried out and through tears saw Yonan waveringly turn from the fire his sword in hand.

The blade plunged down on her wrist. But what followed was not searing torment but cold, icy cold as if she lay in a bank of snow near frozen. And the cold spread from that touch up her arm into her body. She was awake inside the envelope of that flesh and bone but it would not obey her, nor could she even give tongue to ease the torture of the cold.

It withdrew and she felt the return of the fire, all the worse now because of the cold which had produced it. She heard words but they did not mean anything.

"The poison spreads—she will die—" Was that Yonan? Did it matter? Dead—maybe she was already dead or so near that gateway that she was done with struggle.

"Where is your jewel, Lady—?"

"It is not for such a purpose."

"No? You would let her die when you know that she means much to your search?"

"I can search alone—"

"Was that what your council asked of you?"

"You are a man—what do you know of power?"

"Enough to judge that you can use it for more than one thing, Lady. And I say—use it here—and now!"

Once more the cold—the aching numbness returned—she fell down the monster's length—perhaps—but it was all darkness at the bottom.

Fifteen

Kelsie was walking, though it was no more than a weak stumble upheld by the strength of another. When she strove to focus her eyes what she saw just ahead was the swing of a gray robe. Or was it that? Fur? The upheld banner of a cat's tail as that animal, grown to panther size, stalked ahead of her. Cat—there was a cat—and a gate—and after that a wild range of action which one part of her had never accepted as reality. She raised her hand in a gesture which demanded a mighty effort. There was no chain embedded in the flesh about its wrist—but there were scars there which certainly she had never borne before.

"Lady—" from some distance came that call. Kelsie tried to refuse to hear it. Just as she tried to command her legs to halt, to let her rest.

"Lady!"

More strident, demanding. Somehow she made the very great effort to turn her head and look to a face half masked by a war helm. The gray robe tail before her twitched and swirled as its wearer halted and turned to look at her.

"Girl!" there was no concern in that, only demand. "Look to the jewel!"

From somewhere, a third of the way down her weakened body, there came a glow. She dropped her head a little and saw that there was a spot of twirling light on her breast. She moved her scarred hand up to clasp it. Fire! Immediately she dropped her hand—there had been blasting fire before, she wanted none of that again.

"We are followed," those words were spoken over her and meant nothing.

"Can you aid then? What of the jewel, will it not sustain one who wears it?"

"One who wears it rightfully, who does not come to it by the left hand as this one does—perhaps—" Was it the cat who answered? Kelsie really did not care. If they would only leave her alone!

"Let—me—go—" she got out those words with great effort.

She swayed back and forth in the hands of the one who had been leading her, while the cat stood and watched and would have nothing to do with the matter.

"Come—Lady—wake! They sniff behind us and we cannot let them catch up with us."

Her hand batting blindly before her, closed now upon the jewel on her own breast. Then—

She stood in a place where there were many pillars though few of them still supported any remains of roof. The black marks of ancient fires sooted paths up the outer ones. But she had not come here to see the remaining disaster— she had come because she must. There was that which drove on her weakened body. Again in the very far distance she heard voices which had no real meaning:

"Where does she go?"

"Loose her, fool. The drawing of the stone is on her where she goes—that is our road."

There were the pillars and she passed them, but, still, though the outer ones stood behind her there were ranks upon ranks of others reaching to the far distance so she could see no end to the way between them. Once her path tightened to a double line of the stone trees and she saw behind them great chairs of state. Each of those was occupied by a weaving and wreathing of smoke as if what sat there was or could not be wholly fixed in this world. If those shadows of shadows meant her ill they did not move to stop her, nor turn her from the way. On she passed with the burning jewel in her hand and there was nothing left for her but to seek what had been lost and must be found again.

How many miles did that pillar path run? She might have been walking an hour, or a day, and still there was no end. Now there crouched strange and grotesque beasts between the upright columns of stone but none laid paw nor tooth upon her as she slipped on. For she did not seem to be walking any longer, instead she was—

Awake! That waking was sharp, she might have been brought out of sleep by a blow. She knew who she was— who wore that gray robe and now marched to her left, who matched step with her to the right and upheld her body. It was night and the moon, just beginning to wane, brought sharp light and shadow to the ground around her.

They were no longer in a wood but on an open plain where they must be clearly visible to any who followed them and she turned her head to ask of him who so guided her what they did here—

Only she already knew. She must follow where the jewel led. Although she no longer held it cradled in her hand, rather it was stretched forward on its chain, away from her body, she could even feel the fret of the chain against her neck as if it would be free of all anchorage, free to seize its own road and speed to reach what called it so.

There was another bright glow. The other gem, the one worn by Wittle, was also alive but it did not pull against its chain and Kelsie believed its glow was not as great as the one she wore.

"Where are we?" she managed that question and her voice came out more strongly than she had felt it would.

Wittle answered almost breathlessly:

"This is the path you have chosen, yours the answer. Where are we? We have walked through a day and when we rested it was necessary to curb you like a restless horse. We have walked through much of the night. And those who hunt, hunt—yet they bring not their hunt to take us—not yet. You were never wedded to the stone, so how comes it that that jewel takes life as I have never seen before? What do you with it, outlander?"

"I do nothing. It is the stone—"

"They have always told us," Wittle continued as if Kelsie had not spoken at all, "that when a witch dies, so does the power of her stone. Yet Makeease is dead and you who have no right to it are governed by it. This is a thing beyond the bounds of what must be."

Kelsie longed to raise her hand and drag the thing from about her throat, hurl it out into the ocean of tall grass through which they now strode.

"It is no choice of mine—" she said dully.

"This is a thing which—"

"Why keep you on that rack of speech?" Yonan broke in. "You have said it far too many times. It should not be but it is. Therefore accept it."

The witch turned her head and the look which flashed past Kelsie to the warrior was one of pure and blazing anger.

"Be quiet, man. What do your kind know of the mysteries?"

Kelsie had a flash of memory but it was vague as if she watched it happen to another. Of the Quan iron hilt being pressed to the wound in her wrist and then lips sucking— then the cold of a jewel following upon that.

"He won me life," she said out of that memory. "Of what good your spells were then, Wittle? And I think," she was frowning a little, "that we come upon something which is stronger than a jewel." Her head was being bent forward and now the jewel she wore was tugging as if to free itself entirely from her body. Yet she understood in part that were it to vanish along the path it had found for itself she would lose all trace of it. Even the witch's own jewel grew brighter, lifted a little from the gray robe.

The sea of grass tall enough to switch about their knees had been broken by what lay ahead—some shadows which might be heights, save there was no range of mountains—

only a soft rolling as for hills. They were headed directly for that shadowed land.

Twice birds swooped and soared over them—black and red feathers showing up plainly even in the dull light. And, while they made no move toward attack, Kelsie was certain that these were of the Dark, perhaps scouts for the Sarn Riders or those like them. Yet the three of them made no effort toward concealment but headed straight for the hills across the open plain.

Wittle was repeating some words, by the sound of them the same ones over and over. Yonan marched without any comment, but always at her side, close enough to reach out and touch her should some necessity for that arise.

The moon made sharp divisions between light and dark. Here and there a bush grew above the green of the plain and she eyed each of those with apprehension for it seemed to her that the shadows those bushes threw were not like in outline to the shrubs at all but had a curious shifting as if something invisible but still answering the power of the moonlight lurked therein.

A first pale streak of dawn was in the sky when their footing changed. They were not walking over a pavement of half-buried skulls but the grass became thin clumps edging up between blocks of white stone which had undoubtedly once formed a road. And as they fell into step on that rough surface where many of the blocks were uptilted Kelsie became aware of something else. She could not hear nor see, she could only feel it—that greater compulsion, the sense that what must be done must be accomplished quickly, filled her and she began to trot. Wittle and Yonan, after a moment matching her stride for stride.

The road led through a gap in the first line of hills and on either side as they entered that open space there were stone pillars, rough hewn, licked by time into uneven surfaces so that only fragments of what might be designs or patterns remained.

As she passed between these, a little ahead of her two companions, something very far within her stirred. This was certainly not of her own memory but she raised both hands in a salute to the east and to the west. Excitement flashed into life within her.

On ran the road, in better condition here where there was less growth of grass to impinge upon the surface. From the pillars there continued a line of hummocks or small rounded stones, perhaps never meant as walls but to mark more clearly the path. Twice they turned with the road, once right, once left. Then their way was blocked by the rise of a larger hillock straight across its surface. To this Kelsie went, the stone tugging at her as if she were on a leash. Then she found herself spread-eagled against the very side of the earth, the gem a small fire between her breast and the soil against which she involuntarily pressed her body, as if her strength alone could draw her into the earth to seek what the Witch Jewel sought.

She turned her head and looked to Wittle. Her jewel also was now standing away from her body, on a direct line with the hill.

"Within—or beyond," the witch said.

Kelsie found herself digging with crooked fingers at the turf and soil, trying to burrow within as might an animal seeking a den. She saw Wittle's fingers reach out to copy her. Then they were both pulled away and Yonan took their place, hacking with his sword at the covering of the tough-rooted grass. The Quan iron in his hilt was ablaze as Kelsie had not seen it before.

He pried and pulled and there came loose a large slab of soil mixed with roots. Under that, plain to see in the dawn light was stone, streaked and earth stained. He attacked again and again until there was a slab as big as a doorway facing them.

Kelsie gave an involuntary cry. She was pulled forward as her stone fitted itself against that doorway, being thrown to her knees so that the bursting fire of the jewel came where normally there might be a latch. Against that stone, though she tried to tug it away with her hands, or to protect her face from coming in contact with the rough rock, the jewel began to turn, slowly and steadily to the right, twisting its chain and shutting off her breath as if she were being garroted by the silver lengths. She got her hands between her throat and that twisted loop but she could not break its hold upon her, nor free the jewel again from the stone to which it clung.

She cried out in a choking croak for aid and Yonan was beside her, his dagger beating down against the chain. She was gasping for breath when his assault was successful and the chain broke suddenly as she fell gasping, rubbing her throat and drawing in deep lungfuls of air. Then she saw that Wittle had fallen on her knees to take her place. As Kelsie's stone had circled right so did the witch's now plant itself beside the other and turn left.

But, warned by Kelsie's experience, the witch had withdrawn the chain from her throat and now she kept hold but was not prisoner of a choking line of links. Right from top to bottom passed one gem like a hand on a clock face, and on the left the other followed the same pattern. They glowed with a fierce fire so that Kelsie shaded her eyes unable to look upon them.

There was a sucking sound, and then a dull grating. Yonan's hands on her shoulders pulled her back quickly so that, still on her knees, she came up against his legs and now she dared peer between her fingers. There was an opening. The stone slab stood ajar, not open all the way, and somehow in spite of the light in this valley there was utter dark beyond.

"They seek that which there is to be found!" Wittle also on her knees crowded closer. "We have come to what was lost and is now found!"

She held out her hand, passing it through the glow of the two stones and that which was hers loosed itself from its anchorage and fell into her grasp. Reluctantly Kelsie followed her action and once more held the gem, dangling from its broken chain.

If the slit was meant to be a door time had cemented it nearly closed and all three of them tugging together could not bring it open but a fraction more. Wittle at last scraped her way through between the edge of that slab and the frame on which it was set. Once more Kelsie's stone had lifted outward and was in a straight line pointing to the same slit. Nor, she was sure, would it allow her now to step aside. Her body, her feet, moved by another will and, though she longed to hold to that door and allow the chain to go from her with its perilous burden, she again had no chance, her fingers would not unhook from the links.

In Wittle's wake she edged through and, hearing the scrape of metal against stone, knew that Yonan was following. Ahead she saw the sparkling motes and with them the edge of the witch's gray robe but whither they walked she could not tell. Save that there was more of the icy chill she had long ago come to associate with the Dark and the places it haunted.

She smelled earth and stone and there was something else—a feeling that the three of them were not alone—that there was a thing which watched them, not with menace, nor welcome, good will nor ill, but in a kind of dulled awakening.

Wittle's figure suddenly arose and then Kelsie came to the first of a rough-hewn stairs and followed. Though both the jewels were alight, their outer expansion of radiance appeared confined by the dark showing nothing of the walls of this passage or what lay ahead. They came into another passage twin to the one on the level below but at its far end was the gleam of light which was not born of the gems but of the day itself.

They came out on a broad ledge to look down upon a stretch of country which had the appearance of utter desolation. At first Kelsie thought they were above a forest where the trees had been denuded of branches and leaves and only the upstanding trunks left like rows of shattered teeth. Then she realized that these were instead pillars of pitted stone, though there were no signs of what kind of a roof they had once supported—just the gray-white line of rounded columns.

From the ledge a long stairway of badly eroded steps formed an unprotected descent against the side of the cliff and Wittle was already on the first steps of that, headed confidently downward. Kelsie had no recourse but to follow, for the gem in her hand turned and pointed in the direction of the strange ruin below.

That filled completely a valley of some size and triangular shape. They were in the narrow end of the triangle. Kelsie could guess that what had once been erected here was of great importance in its day—temple, palace, fortress, whatever it had been.

They passed from the steps directly onto a pavement in which the columns were rooted. It was not the universal gray of the pillars but a blue which was nearly green—so at a distance one might even believe that it was a stretch of turf. This in turn was patterned in a brighter blue with signs or symbols which formed intricate arabesques under their feet, though here and there wind-driven patches of soil had blown in to cover the lines. There were no marks in such dust, no sign that any had been here before them through long quiet years.

Again Kelsie found no trace of that Dark which chilled body and spirit. Nor in fact anything but the vague impression that something very deeply asleep was waking at their coming, and, had she had the power of controlling her own body, she would have raced back up those stairs and out through the passage to a world more normal than this.

If she had suspicions, Wittle did not share them. Instead the witch marched forward with a rapt expression of expectation on her face. Thus they paraded down one of the aisles between columns, Wittle in advance, Kelsie on her heels, Yonan bringing up the rear. He kept his sword unsheathed and ready—either because he had come to depend upon the Quan iron in the hilt or because he actually feared that they would meet active opposition sooner or later.

Between the columns they could see the walls of the valley gradually opening out wider and wider, the pillars arranged so that one could be sure that this erection had covered the whole of the valley floor at one time. Unlike the building in which the monster dwelled there was no vibration, no sense of any life save their own. Not until they were well away from the place where they had entered the forest of stone trees.

One of the drifts of soil which had entered here and there to carpet over the blue stone lay across their path. Wittle showed no intention of halting but Yonan pushed beside Kelsie and actually caught at the wide sleeve of the witch's robe, bringing her to a sudden stop. With his sword the warrior pointed to that stretch of earth.

Pressed deeply into its surface were tracks. Kelsie was sure that the most clear, which overlaid others mingled before, were those of a bare foot that looked human. Wittle tried to free herself from Yonan's hold with a sharp pull. Her mask of expectancy cracked and it was with fiery anger she looked to him.

"What do you?" Her harsh voice scaled up and awoke echoes as if behind a myriad of those columns stood other Wittles to add their demands to hers.

"Look!" Again he indicated the tracks. "These are fresh—see where the soil yet crumbles into the impression. We are not alone here, Lady. Would you march to a meeting and take no heed of what may await us ahead?"

She gestured to the aisle before her. "Do you see aught to dispute us here, warrior? I say again—try not to deal with what no man may understand!"

"Perhaps we understand more than you would allow us, Witch," he said with a spark of anger in his reply. "Did you not agree that we may have been allowed to escape so that we might be traced to that which you revere so mightily—a source of the true power? If some trap has been laid ahead we shall be the better for suspecting it."

She had cupped her stone in her two hands and now held it up to breathe upon it. Her lips moved but they could not hear what she said—a ritual, Kelsie suspected. The gem flared higher and then its radiance, which had been growing as they marched forward, disappeared. It looked to the girl as if instead of a jewel Wittle held a palm full of water and was brooding over it.

There was change in her own stone also and she hastened to examine it. Though the beam it had given off so far had been white with a tinge of blue now it became fully blue— as clear and welcome as a fair day in midsummer, cloudless and promising a fine day. Then a shadow crossed it and she saw as plainly as if she stood before them the form of the wildcat, her two kittens, and the snow cubling she had adopted. They lay in the warm sun on a rock, the cat nursing all three of her family, her eyes half closed in her own contentment. But, even as Kelsie watched those eyes opened and were raised, as if the animal saw her in this place and time. Then the picture shivered and was gone.

Cat? What had the wildcat to do with her here and now. She remembered that the stone she held had not been a direct gift from the dying witch but had come through the cat. And—she looked down at that footprinted reach of soil on the floor. Yes! Now that she looked carefully she could see those other tracks—the sign of one of the feline family crossing beneath the barefooted prints. Cat—she had never seen any in this valley save the one who had brought this whole adventure on her. Familiars—the old stories from her own world of how cats had consorted with those deemed witches in the past. What had cats to do with this place here and now?

Wittle looked up from her own jewel. "There is no trace of the Dark here!" she exclaimed.

"And of the Light?" Yonan persisted.

The witch hesitated as if she weighed truth against falsehood in order to gain her own ends. Then she admitted reluctantly:

"Nor of that either."

"But of power?" he persisted. She gave him a look of true hatred.

"There is power—power can exist without Dark or Light." Kelsie thought Wittle spoke as if to reassure herself. "Many were the adepts who drew upon neither but strove for pure knowledge alone. Our records speak of such. We may now be approachng a place where such neutral power can be tapped. If we reach there," her eyes glistened and there was a small bubble of saliva at one corner of her thin-lipped mouth, "then we can claim it for the Light. If the Dark reaches it first then—"

"Then you would say all is lost? But have you any thought as to what has already sought it according to this trail?" For the second time he pointed his sword to the tracks.

She leaned over that stretch of soil and deliberately allowed her jewel to swing low, nearly touching the disturbed earth. There was no change in its color now, and it halted on the outward swing, still pointing to whatever lay ahead of them.

She favored Yonan with a malicious smile. "Do you mark this, warrior? There is no harm."

He did not sheath his sword but met her eye to eye. "I do not question any power, Witch—yours or those of the Dark we have left behind. But mark this, you may be intruding upon something which even all the learning in Lormt does not now hold. It is best to go wary—"

"Do you go wary!" she snapped. "What man can know unless he is shown—as you will be shown when the time comes!"

And she deliberately stepped on the barefooted track as she started on.

Sixteen

The rows of columns stopped abruptly. Though on the other side of the deep gap now facing them, Kelsie saw more continuing for stiff, endless miles. However, there was no bridge. Wittle, who had been so intent on their journey that she had watched her jewel far more than she had watched her footing, teetered on the brink of a drop until Yonan swept her back.

They stood together then looking down into another world, or was it the same they had known and they had soared above it? Were they now so mighty of body, so long of sight that they were giants who could cross a land with three or four crushing strides? For what they saw below was a miniature landscape, and a second later Yonan was on his knees hanging over the edge.

"The Valley!" he cried out, "and the mountains of the west—Estcarp . . . Escore!"

The witch swung her stone or it was being swung for her. Her eyes were piercingly bright in her narrow face. "Lormt . . . Es—"

It was indeed a country in miniature. There were mountains raised herein which, seen this way, equaled peaks, there were flowing rivers, and lakes, and the bold stand of keeps and villages, a city or two—forests and glades, plains and highlands. There were circles of upstanding stones and other markings raised by the power of men—or more than men. Yet all of this seemed to center about one huge building in the center of the miniature landscape, a building which was roofless, open to the sky and which might be the one they stood within. Therein was another hollow and in it another miniature world yet smaller, and in that another columned place and a third road.

Kelsie shook her head to cure her dizziness. All this was like one of those confusing paintings in which there was a second painting and inside of that another and so on until there was a final dot too small to distinguish clearly. Thinking that, she looked up into the light of early day to see if there *were* walls about them and if they were, in turn, part of a larger world.

Both Wittle's jewel and her own had swung out over that small world and now jerked against the hold kept upon them. They might live and move by a purpose beyond human reckoning. Kelsie loosed hers. It sped out across the miniature world until it hung above that second columned temple, over the second miniature world, and up toward it lanced a gleam of light from the center of that world. The jewel became like a sun burning with such brilliance that Kelsie was forced to shade her eyes. Wittle, through carelessness or desire, had loosed her stone also and it was winging its way toward the same place. There was a shattering, a brilliant light which appeared, not in the miniature of their world, but over their own heads. Then fell a rain of slivered crystal, each piece rainbow bright about them. Though none fell on them or did them harm.

Yet there was also a ringing, a trilling, as of crystal bits set swinging against each other in the breeze. It was a singing which began in high joyfulness but which declined, as Kelsie listened raptly to the music, to more somber notes. Also now there were patches of shadow which flowed across the small world. Here and there it was dark where there had been light and the dark grew wider and thicker. Until perhaps a third of the small world was enshadowed. While more and more somber grew the crystal music.

Kelsie found herself stretching forth her hands as if to sweep away the nearest of those shadows, to awaken once more the brilliant light. She discovered that she could not distinguish her crystal from that which had come from Wittle's hold, for they spun together in a ball, fighting the shadows with the sparkling light they threw. Their light completely held that second miniature world free of the dark, though Kelsie knew as well as if she could see it that the shadows attempted to override that world also.

Wittle was on her knees and from her lips poured words in rhythm which could only be a spell or a song. While Kelsie found herself also singing in notes which fitted the tinkling of the crystal:

> "Light to Dark,
>   Dark to light
>   After Day comes the night
>   After night the morning clear
>   Hope rises always from all fear!"

She saw Wittle hold out her hands to summon back her jewel but it did not come. Tears she had never expected to see the witch shed ran from her eyes down to soak the bosom of her gray robe.

Kelsie also knew a sense of loss so great that it darkened for her all the wonder which she watched. Her singing dwindled to a sob and then another. But she did not reach for that which she had never wanted but which had become a part of her.

Now that battlefield between Light and Dark became more vividly defined, more broken, cutting one side of the country below from another. The darker bits grew darker. Yet the jewels which formed the light of that world continued to spin. Where their sparks fell the Dark retreated. Though, as they spun also, villages were deserted and fell into ruin, the very shape of the country changed. Mountains danced to the somber sounds of the crystal and were raised and twisted. Only here and there did the light hold bright and clear.

Kelsie knew that what she looked upon had happened and this had been the fate of this land. But though it changed she saw no people—only the growth and the ebb of the jewel light. Now that light was growing again as if the faster it whirled the more power it was drawing toward it.

She took heart as she saw one shadow fade, another break suddenly into bits as if it were tangible and could be so handled.

Then—

Out from the columns on the other side of this world-in-the-small came a beam of fierce red to strike full upon the whirling crystals of the jewels. Their clear light clouded— what was white and gold became red and darkened. The shadows on the surface of the world took heart, gathered, spread, ate up more and more of the land. Kelsie cried out wretchedly for she knew that in loosing her gem here she had given an opening to the Dark which was avidly seizing upon it.

She leaned perilously over the edge of the miniature country and tried now to reach some part of her jewel, one of the flying ends of chain if that were possible. Only it was far beyond her touch. She heard Wittle give a great cry and saw her crumple up and lie, one arm swinging down to brush the top of one of the mountains below.

"To me!" Did Kelsie cry that aloud or only shape the call with her whole body? As she had done before, she willed her strength to the spinning jewel. It was not hers, it had never been hers by right, but it had served her before and now she was determined it should not vanish into darkness and defeat.

Into it she aimed her thought, all her will. She saw it spin as it had, she would hold to that picture in her mind no matter what happened. Spin it must—for if it faltered it would be gone, all the power within it to feed the Dark which would grow a hundredfold from such a feasting. She willed—and willed—

A hand dropped upon her shoulder and from that touch she greedily drew more strength. She only half saw, so intent was she upon the battle in the pit, that Yonan was between her and Wittle, that his right hand rested on her, his left was on the witch. She drew and from him came the energy and she willed—oh, how she willed. Yet one part of her, small and far withdrawn, wondered at what she did and how she knew what was to be done.

The red was an angry fire and more and more the clear light of the jewels was swallowed up. Yonan's hand was gone from her shoulder, she was no longer a part of that linkage which had given her the energy to go on fighting. She saw the warrior running, skirting the rim of that pit which held the miniature world. He was heading for the source of the red beam. That musical tinkling which had been a part of the meeting of the jewels was drowned out by a thumping which reminded her of the vibration in the mountainous monster, of the drums of the Thas. Still she struggled to hold alive her jewel, to feed it with her will.

Wittle stirred, levered herself up with her hands. Her face was drawn and she looked as if dozens of years had racked her during the space while she had lain there. But once more her lips were moving soundlessly and Kelsie believed that she was reciting the ritual which was a part of her witch training.

There came a distant shouting, the clashing of arms. Yonan—he must have won to the enemy! Though Kelsie thought there was little he could do there. Then a shout which overran the drum sound—

"Glydys—Ninutra!"

While Wittle, now on her knees, cried out:

"By the will of Langue, by the power of Thresees, by the memory of Janderoth!"

Those they called upon or evoked had no meaning for Kelsie—she had only that determination not to yield. Again that small part of her wondered why it was so important that she win. What was this world to her? Yet the rest of her quivered and shrank as she watched the shadow spread.

But was it spreading? She was sure that a finger of the dark which had been aimed across one corner to reach a cape stretching out into a strange sea was withdrawing. From that cape itself, there roused a spark of fire which burned blue. There was another blue fire burning also, closer to her, and its flame was clear. The twin suns which were the jewels spun on and the blood-red haze about them was fading a little.

Kelsie concentrated on that and tried to put out of her mind those sounds of battle which came from the other side of the world basin. These people called upon their gods, their forms of power. What had she to call upon save what was in her?

She snarled without knowing that her lips shaped that sound, there was anger deep within her, an anger she did not understand but which heated her as had that first flash of protest which had led to her coming through the gate. Just as she would not witness the death of an animal, so now she refused to witness the death of a world. For the miniature land beneath had become as real to her now as what lay outside the columns of stone.

NO! She did not shout any petition of gods nor battle cries, she just poured in her will. Perhaps Wittle did that also, for now the gems spun so fast that they formed a single ball of fire. The red beam lapped around it but it could not cut off that burst of radiance, subdue it.

The shouting came from her right now. Yonan might be forced back by a superior force. Yet the red beam began to pulsate, its strength interrupted and broken from time to time. There—when it died next—will—use the will! And so she did.

That red beam no longer struck at the jewels, it strove to aim straight down at the miniature world—its force seeking out that spark of blue which was on the sea—and the other on the land. The jewels whirled into dazzling brilliance and sparks flowed and sprang from their action. This patterned out across the world, and where they struck new blue flames arose. The shadows flinched back from those, and began to dart here and there striving to douse each spark before it started a new fire burning.

A clashing of swords. Kelsie, torn from her concentration, looked to her right. Yonan was being forced back right enough. Engaging him were two manlike figures and a creature which might have been out of a nightmare. Yet he parried and thrust as if he had erected such a wall of steel many times before.

"The jewel—hold—the jewel!" Wittle had broken her chant and was close to the girl, raking painfully down Kelsie's arm with crooked fingers.

Yes—the jewel. She looked back to the battle over the basin world. And her folly brought a gasp from her. For one of the gems was spinning slower and slower, there were no more sparks cast off to start those alternate fires on the ground below. The red beam of light no longer strove to battle the jewels and their sparks, instead it raised, struck straight at Wittle, at her.

It was like being caught within a wave of liquid filth. All that was cruel, wrong, seedlings of evil in her own nature answered that red beam. Now Kelsie had to fight—not that—but what lay within herself. All the small meannesses which she had ever been capable of and had yielded to arose in her memory, all her failures and self-doubts near overwhelmed her. What was she doing here risking her life and perhaps more than mere physical life, in this battle? She had no reason to defend a world into which she was not born, with which she had no ties. No, that jewel she had cherished belonged to a dead woman, a woman who had suffered the same penalty for her foolhardiness that Kelsie was about to have visited on her.

She had no powers such as Wittle and all the rest had prated of ever since she had arrived here. What was she trying to do?

That small part of her which had doubled and scoffed throughout all the days and nights she had traveled thrust aside barriers in her mind and came to her. She need only rise, let go her tenuous tie with the jewel, and she could walk out of here in freedom—no, in more than freedom, for those of the other side offered gifts—

Their gifts! Perhaps they might have won her but they went too far and showed her their bribes. If she did nothing here which was to their harm why should they offer more than to let her withdraw from the field? She shook her head against their mind pictures, no longer subtle—no longer dealing with her own thoughts and fears. She saw images slipping by so fast she could hardly seize upon any of the individual pictures. Did she want to rule—be sure there would be a throne for her. Did she want treasures—a wavery picture of such floated there. Did she want revenge—cruel and bloody pictures flashed by. Did she want this world before her to play with, to change to her fancy, to hold its whole destiny—to—

Her will arose again and fastened upon the slower spinning jewel. She was no witch, this power had been lent her second-hand. But neither did she want what had been offered her. Will it—will the end of that other—that which was the red flame now ringing her about, its heat reaching for the seeds of her anger and striving to turn them toward its own goal.

She did not know if similar temptations had been thrown at Wittle, though she was sure that she had seen the other jewel also falter for an instant or two. But the witch had been long lessoned in what she did. Perhaps those who spun that web had built it for the people of this world, and the very fact that Kelsie was not born of it was not a weakness but a strength.

The gems spun on as the red beam closed around both women. It was more than a mind goad now; heat came from it searing her flesh as if she were thrust into a fire. And that pain was the final key which set Kelsie free of any temptation which might have moved her. She set her teeth and held to the jewel, concentrating upon it with all her might. Power as Wittle understood it she might not have.

But perhaps that which she had brought with her was as solid and steadfast in its own way.

The spin no longer faltered but grew swifter and the sparks it once more flung off were brighter. Down in the basin world shadows retreated. Here and there a fresh blue glow answered from newly-freed land. She felt the concentration of the red fire building up and knew that while it still tried to disrupt the power of the jewels it was now also being bent toward her in a last frenzy of battle. She could have screamed under the lash of that heated beam but she did not—to her own growing wonder she held. Kelsie saw Wittle begin to lever herself up from the stone, her gaunt face turned toward the spinning gems.

Suddenly, instead of trying only to hold to her own, Kelsie tried to fight back—to actually aim those sparks of cleansing light to the portions of the basin where the darkest of the shadows clung in a noisome and threatening mist. The blue glows elsewhere grew stronger, spread. There! Exultation filled her—she had actually placed a spark where she willed and, though it was dimmed by the dark, it was not forced into oblivion. It remained. There came another not far away.

"Ninatur!" Through the concentration which held her she held her control though Yonan was being forced back toward them. There were crumpled forms, both human and monstrous, marking the path of his retreat, and blood dripped from sheared mail on his own side. But still he was buying them time. Time for what? How long could they hold their jewels and defeat the semblance of the dark? No—any doubt weakened her control—she must concentrate on what spun out there above the basin land.

The red haze thickened. Yonan was hidden from her; even Wittle was only a shadow within the bloody fog. But that could not hide the flash of the jewels nor the fact that the shadows were in retreat from that light.

"Die then!"

The threat may only have touched her mind, spun out of the fog, but it was like a shout to awaken echoes from her very bones. In an instant the red beam loosened its struggle with the jewels, was shot straight to where she and Wittle carried on their part of this strange duel.

"Die!"

She was gasping for clean air, her lungs filled instead with thick flaming gas. Yet that was not true, another part of her proclaimed. This was the last weapon of the shadow—and where was her weapon—out there!

She held to her thought of the jewel, unable to see it now that the thick haze wrapped her round. Hold—only hold—

Past her will there worked another order which she could not contain and defeat. Fight! Aim the jewel not toward the land she had guarded but down the beam of the red curtain—strike so a blow of her own. The gem answered to that impulse. No longer did it spin and weave its own kind of protection above the world in miniature—instead it wavered on its axes and then settled into a sharp pattern of its own, speeding down the ray of red which formed a guide. It hurled its way as she might have thrown a stone full force. From it came a whining note, rising ever higher and higher, until she could no longer hear it, only feel it throughout her body.

But Wittle's jewel held in place though it threw off no more of the life inducing sparks and the shadows began to gather once again. On sped the star which was Kelsie's borrowed stone. There was no sight of it by eye anymore; only in her mind could she follow its furious pace. Around her the fierce lash of the heat was beginning to fail—whoever had raised that was indrawing all strengths, preparing for a final battle. She felt no lack of confidence. Instead a fierce pride and exultation. As if by carrying battle to the enemy she had doomed her own cause.

"Ninatur!" Again came Yonan's war cry out of the ruddy dusk, seeming farther away. Kelsie crouched, her whole sense of will and strength concentrated on the disappearing jewel.

She had a vision which dazzled even her open eyes, causing her to blink. There was a single figure on the other side of the basin. She could not see it clearly, but she had a mind picture of a gleaming white body twisting and turning as if in some strange formal dance. From each footfall on the stone there came a new puff of red to fit itself into the stream of the beam. But the jewel had reached there and come to hang over the dancer's head.

Kelsie threw forth in that moment all her strength of will. The jewel steadied, began to spin as it had above the land in the basin. Now she could mind see it, now she could not as another blast of red fumes arose. But she sensed something else—that the dancer had not expected this, that it must take time to recall the strength of the beam in self-defense. That time must not be allowed. As she had struck sparks by will from the star in the basin, so Kelsie now tried to gain the same from the spin of the jewel in that place the Shadow's servant believed safe. Round—so! Round again!

She felt as if the beam were searing her to her very bones yet there was that in her which would not recall the miniature sun which now fought her battle beyond the reach of eyesight. Turn—spark—spark! There!

A first speck of light broke from that encircling brilliance about the jewel. The flying feet of the dancer were fashioning a new pattern, one which must not be allowed to become a form. There—another spark and the dancer faltered for a single instant, less than a breath out of time. But faltered it had! Now!

With all the strength she could summon up Kelsie aimed her second blow. And perhaps her last. She was so wrapped up in the haze that she felt she was completely encased from the real world, entrapped in this torment. Perhaps the mind picture she held to was also an illusion and she was being tricked.

There was a tremor down the beam which closed her in so. And then a second one. She could breathe without those torturing rasps for throat and lungs. Her spirit arose. Yes! The dancer was not so sure of the pattern now—there were sparks—not as great as those which the jewel had flung into the basin world but enough to cut through the web the other wove, to loosen here and there some portion of the intended design. Now!

Kelsie threw herself to the left, rolled over the rock until her body thudded against that of Wittle. One hand lashed out and tightened about the witch's bony shoulder.

"Give me power!" Kelsie may not have shouted that cry but it rang through her body. Perhaps the very suddenness of it made Wittle obey. Through her hand upon the other came a surge of strength and in the girl's mind the jewel began a wider swing, following the dancer in and out, emitting a shower of sparks which struck downward.

Kelsie felt as if she were swelling through her own body—that what she gathered in from Wittle was too great to be held or she herself would be consumed—and she fought to channel it in her mind—aim it toward that other world weapon she could not see.

The red curtain enclosing the two of them began to diffuse; she could see the witch now—though Wittle had not turned her head nor made any gesture to suggest that she saw Kelsie. Wittle's gaze strained instead out over the basin. There, very dim in the red of the slowly disrupting beam was her own jewel—still suspended in the air but no longer spinning so swiftly, rather wobbling as if what supported it was nearly gone.

But Kelsie had no mind for that—the battle moved across and they must defeat the dancer not the again growing shadows over the smaller world.

"Release—send!" demanded the girl. "Give strength—"

She could still feel the inflow from her hold upon the witch but it was lessening. Her mind picture of the dancer grew hazier and hazier until she could not be sure that that other existed at all, that she had not been drawn into a trap which had finished both the jewels and left the basin world open to the Dark.

Seventeen

There was dark, a fume filled, suffocating darkness and in that still moved the dancer though the lightsome patter of feet had become a desperate shuffle. Then—nothing—

Kelsie opened her eyes. She lay by the edge of the basin and near her was a heap of travel-stained gray which would only be Wittle. From far overhead came the faint crystalline music she had first heard when the jewels had been loosed over the miniature world. With an effort she turned her head, edged toward the verge of the basin. The red wave was gone and afar there twisted and turned a single jewel—Wittle's, she thought. Her hand sought her own breast somehow hoping that she had not lost what had seemed to be a burden she had never asked to carry but which had become a part of her.

"Yonan?" she called in a voice which sounded cracked from the ordeal of the heat. There was no answer. She got to her knee then and started to search toward where she had had the single sight of him during the battle. There were bodies there—two of them—one in mail.

Somehow she got to her feet and lurched in that direction. There was an emptiness about her as if something had withdrawn or been banished from that world within a world. Not only her jewel, she thought.

Past those bodies she tottered, stooping to make sure that

he in the mail was not the Valley warrior. But it was a dark, cruel face which met her gaze. She skirted well by the monster having no desire to see it the closer.

There were splashes of blood on the stones and she kept to that trail. Where her jewel had gone, that was where she must go also. Though she already knew that she had no talisman, no weapon she could now claim.

A third body mail clad, lying face down. She made herself stoop and lift the head, turn it to look upon more strange features. Where was Yonan? She lifted her voice and called aloud his name which came in echoes back from the world of the basin. On she plodded, now working her way from the support of one pillar to that of the next. More blood, a hacked body of a monster thing all hair and talons. Then she could see a little ahead.

Someone sat, back to a column, head fallen forward on his breast.

"Yonan!" she pushed away from the pillar she had just embraced and stumbled on. There was blackened stone here, and the stench of fire-seared flesh. Yet she was sure she had seen a movement in the one who was seated. She had almost reached his side when she saw that other. Crumpled as if all strength of body had been withdrawn in a single instant lay a child!

Nausea arose in Kelsie. Among the bodies, half seared, half flame eaten, those white limbs were intact with no sign of the fire which must have exploded here.

The man by the pillar turned his head slowly. Yonan! She had found him in truth. His sword, the blade snapped off raggedly a handsbreadth from the point, lay beside his empty hand. In the hilt the Quan iron was dulled, spotted black like a fruit in decay.

He raised his head a little to look at her. For the first time she saw a slow smile move his lips, striking years from his somber face.

"You are hurt?" She stood over him uncertainly, knowing nothing of the healing arts for men, only those which she had used with animals. But now she knelt and strove to free him from the blood-stained mail to get at the wound in his side.

With fumbling fingers he tried to help her. Then she uncovered a gaping slit in his flesh which bled sluggishly. From her shift she tore a strip and bandaged him as best she could, using the very last of the powdered illbane which had clung to the inner seams of his own belt wallet to spread upon the stout cloth before she wound it about him.

He lay passive under her hands now, his eyes closed, that curious youth which had touched him earlier all the more plain, so that she could no longer see him as the self-contained scout who had led and protected them, but only a young man who had fought with raw courage to advance a quest which had only been half-possible from the first.

When she had made him as comfortable as she could, curiosity, a fearful and half-ashamed curiosity, brought her to the white figure who lay so still. A fair body of a very young girl, dark hair streaming to conceal her face. Her bare feet so small—surely matching the track they had seen before. Still there was something about her— Was this the dancer who had sought to make an end to the jewels—to them?

Though she shrank from it she made herself uncover the face of the dead, lifting away a heavy strand of the hair. Beauty, yes, and yet with a subtle marking of evil, though Kelsie did not know how or why she judged that. There was the tinkle of crystal and, peering more closely, she saw that on the arm, on the white skin of the dead, was a shifting of small bits of crystal—one or two still alight with a faint bluish glow. The jewel! Again Kelsie knew a pain of loss. Never hers, yet she had borne it and dared to use it. And it had been her final burst of will which had killed this child, brought an end to a battle and—what else had it done?

She went to the rim of the basin and looked down.

Wittle's jewel still spun, slowly, but from it emitted sparks of blue which fell to the world and she saw that the shadows had not altogether been banished but had withdrawn into somber pools of dark here and there and seemed fewer and smaller.

Wittle had come to find power. In a manner it had found her and made use of her—as well as of Kelsie. What they had accomplished here the girl could not understand—maybe it would take an adept such as the people so often spoke of to measure what had been done and whether for good or ill.

"It was an eftan." Yonan spoke for the first time as she turned away from the inner world. "They had suborned an eftan to their purposes."

"An eftan?"

"An air elemental," he explained. "They who can dance up a storm if they wish. And this one danced on the pattern set there—" He pointed to the pavement which was so blackened and scarred around which lay the bodies of the dead save for her who rested inside.

Rested inside?

There was a faint line or two still to be seen on the stone. But— Kelsie put both her hands to her mouth and held back a scream. The white body—it was dissolving—tendrils of whitish smoke from a fire were curling from beneath it. Now she saw the dark disappear, a blast of chill—as from the edge of a mountain snowfield spread outward as the smoke gathered into a long finger. She shrank back a step or two waiting for that ice to thrust at her—to freeze her where the others had burnt from the fire.

But around the white there was a tinge of blue and the smoke arose straight up into the sky above the roofless columns, streaking outward like a thing suddenly released from captivity. Then it was gone and all that lay there was the tiny shreds of crystal.

"What—?" she found it hard to frame proper words. Surely the dancer had died.

"Back to its own place," Yonan said and grimaced, his hand going to his side. "Maybe it was spell-held to what it did here and is now free. Those of its kind seldom mix in the affairs of men—or of demons—" And he glanced at one of the fire-scorched bodies which lay near him.

"Will it come back?" she demanded. "The jewel—it is broken."

"I do not think we shall see that weapon again," he replied, "which does not mean that they will not try other ways." And his grimace grew as he reached for his broken sword, looking from the break to the discolored Quan iron. "We seem to be singularly weaponless now, my lady."

"There is Wittle's jewel—"

"If it still answers her; if she wishes it so—" he did not sound very confident.

"Can you walk?" Her own question sounded harsh and demanding. But she did not want to leave the witch alone. To have their mismatched party all together was her object for the present.

"I am not to be counted out yet, Lady," he made answer and struggled to get arms under him to lever himself up. She was quick to aid. At his gesture she sheathed what was left of his sword and slung the battered coat of mail over her shoulder, placed her arm about him so that they made a slow journey back around the edge of the basin, moving from one pillar to the next and halting many times when she saw the drops of sweat on his forehead, the set of his mouth, as if the last thing he would ask was a slower pace or perhaps a longer rest.

Before they reached her Kelsie heard Wittle's voice. The witch was singing, hoarsely and with a crack in the rhythm of her words. She sat, they could see, on the very edge of the basin, not looking down at the land beneath her but rather out at the slow spinning jewel. And as she so sang she reached out her hands as if to cup it again and hold it unharmed against all comers. There was an avid hunger in her face, the eyes which watched the distant jewel were as deep sunken in her head as if she had been fever-ill for a long time. She paused in her song now and then to rub her forehead with her hands, pressing her fingers on her eyes as if to clear away some film to enable her to see what she wanted to see—that which was a part of her winging its way back into her hold.

Yet the jewel did not pause in its turning, nor change a fraction of its stance. It was playing a strange new sun to the basin world, one seemingly as fixed as might be an actual fire globe in Escore's own sky, the warmth of which reached them now between the pillars.

"Wittle," Kelsie released Yonan against the nearest column and went to put her hands on the witch's bent shoulders. "Wittle!"

She might have been calling now upon the wind or upon that tongue of frosty air which had formed the dancer who had so nearly put an end not only to them but also the world in the basin.

"Wittle!"

The witch swept out one arm, catching Kelsie at thigh height nearly spilling her into the basin. Looking down and out over the miniature world Kelsie could see that there was still a fleeing of shadow, a rain of sparks sending that into nothingness here and there.

"She is one with her jewel," Yonan's voice behind her sounded as if from a distance. "She will be one with it to the end."

"But I—that other jewel—" protested Kelsie.

"You are no witch, at least not one of Estcarp where the power is one with the person. If she recalls her jewel, then she is safe. But if it comes not to her urging—"

"We must get away!" Kelsie had thrown off most of the spell which had been woven about her. With the gem she had carried now nothing but splinters, she felt oddly naked, weaponless, prey to be easily hunted down. And she could not believe that they had indeed defeated that which had striven to destroy not only them but all that lay in the basin.

Now she looked and saw the Valley—of that she was sure. And there were other places where the blue of the Light promised comfort and safety. She began to study the miniature land carefully to see where was the nearest of those islands of true safety. The place of columns as it was in the basin seemed unduly large in comparison with the rest of the countryside. And to the north of that was one of the darkest blots of shadow—though that had been driven back in upon itself she was sure. Originally it had reached out to touch upon the place of pillars. But if she could not rouse Wittle from her trance, nor support Yonan for long, then how could she—

"Get away?" her own earlier words repeated back to her. "Think you we are now meant to get away?" Yonan's voice was low and very tired. She glanced at him quickly. He had slumped farther down against the pillar and now lay there, all color faded from his face so that his weather tan looked gray and dulling.

Kelsie's chin came up and she looked at him straightly. "So far we have won—"

"One battle in a war," he answered her slowly and closed his eyes. Wittle, meanwhile, regarded nothing but the spinning jewel to which her hands still stretched, her crooning now reduced to a hoarse whisper. Kelsie looked out over the bowl. Her stubbornness would not allow her to accept the defeat which seemed to have fallen on Yonan, the entranced state of the witch. She settled down on the rim of the basin and began a survey threaded from the place of columns back toward the Valley. That they would come again to any great source of power such as Wittle sought she did not believe. The compulsion which had carried her on and on to this very place was gone with her—or Roylane's jewel. There was retreat which could save them. If they left the columns here and went so—a little farther west—there was a river and she could trace there to within a short distance of the Valley. Surely once they were back into patrolled territory they would be found, taken back.

"Wittle," she moved along until she knelt by the witch again and now she took her by the shoulders and shook her so hard the woman's head flopped back and forth on her shoulders— "Wittle!"

The dark eyes stared through her as if she were as bodiless as smoke. Nothing she could do would rouse the witch from her need and longing for the jewel. But Kelsie was not through. Now she slapped that lean face hard, on one cheek and then the other so that the print of her hand began to show in reddened patches.

This time there was a flicker in the eyes, the straight stare was broken.

"Wittle!" Under her hands the witch's body twisted as the woman attempted to see beyond Kelsie to the spinning jewel. Now the sparks from that had become fewer and fewer, only a handful were spilled to hunt the shadows out of the corners in which they lay.

"Wittle, they will be hunting us. We must go."

"By Hofer and Tem, by the ten lights, and the nine cups, the six faggots and the three fires—" Her words were understandable but they made no sense to the girl. Wittle raised a hand and drove it finger straight for Kelsie's face, aiming at her eyes. The girl ducked and lost her hold on the witch.

Wittle arose then, the strength of her body such that she had no trouble in tearing away from Kelsie. She took two steps forward, over the edge of the basin.

Kelsie screamed, Wittle was gone. She might have stepped through a door when she had taken that stride forward. There was no sign of her body crashing on the mountains of that other world. At the same time the jewel picked up speed where it hung in the air, whirled twice as fast, threw off a greater volume of sparks. It might have been that Wittle's act had revived it.

"She—she's gone!" Kelsie swept her hand forward where moments earlier the witch had stood. Nothing but air, not even the traces of something such as the eftan had given off in its going.

"Her power was her—" Yonan said, in a tired, fading voice. "When it would not come to her, then she went to it. She has found what she came for—the final consuming power."

As if in answer to his comment the jewel was indeed

ablaze—almost as bright as it had been when Kelsie's jewel had joined with it in splendor. The shadows—they were fleeing, racing back to certain dark places. Even those, one after another, were vanishing to become spaces bare of the blots of evil which had held some of them for so long.

A source of greater power—that was what the witches of Estcarp had sought and that was what Wittle had found.

Kelsie turned to Yonan. That whirling ball of light out there was frightening. If her own jewel had endured would she, too, have been so drawn into it? Could she be influenced now by Wittle's?

She edged back from the basin.

"You were not sealed," Yonan's words meant little to her. She wanted nothing as much as to run down an aisle of those columns, to get out of this place. "You are not a witch out of Estcarp. The jewel came to you as a gift, not a weapon—"

"A gift," she repeated. Such a gift as no one would welcome— "Who would want such as that?" She gestured to the miniature sun the gem had become.

"Many," he returned shortly. There was a shadow across his face, not a reflection of evil but rather one of loss. "To each there are given gifts. Those which we cherish grow." His hand sought his sword belt, closed about the hilt of that broken blade. "I knew another who was offered much and claimed it. She walks now other roads, nor does she remember much of what was before, except as something which is far off and has no longer any connection with her. Glydys," his voice lingered over that name as if he would call its wearer to appear to them now.

But Kelsie was not interested in things of the past. She had retreated so that the rise of a pillar was between her and the whirling sun-stone. For she could not rid herself of the belief that if she remained directly in its light it could also draw her who had so long carried and used its fellow.

"Let us go!" she demanded of Yonan.

His smile was crooked. "Go indeed, Lady. Though I do

not think that evil will hunt now. For me," he raised his hand in a small gesture which indicated his sprawling body, "I need two legs which will carry me."

He was right. For him to rise and retreat down that long way between columns would be perhaps impossible. If they went together they would continue to be exposed to what was here for a long time—maybe too long a time. Yet Kelsie could not take the first step which would take her away to leave him there alone.

"What shall we do?" he asked the question which hung in her own mind but which she would not allow herself to voice. "Why, it is simple, Lady. You go for help, I remain—"

"To face that again?" she waved toward the opposite side of the basin and the scorched dead which lay there. He might have been cut to pieces there had not her own jewel played a hand in the final battle. Final battle? How could she judge that that had already passed? She thought of the hounds, the Sarn Riders, the dead monsters she had seen.

Nor could she believe that the single sun-gem would expend itself beyond the place where it now hung to protect either of them now.

"They have failed," Yonan answered. "Whatever they would have done here is ended. As long as that blazes they are driven back. For I think that this world below us is the mirror image of what surrounds us, and what Wittle has set in motion is for good instead of ill. No, get you gone, Lady—and bring help—"

Instead of answering him she deliberately made herself approach the rim of the basin once more and there stand to trace out what she was sure was the reflection of the Valley, noting the distances between that and the place of columns. With a horse they might have done it—but any horses hereabouts would be those fell beasts of the Riders. It might take her days and she had no surety of keeping to any road when she left here—especially one which led by the keep of the squatting monster.

The Valley. Yes, she could trace it from where she stood.

It was . . . right there!

Out of it now arose something which was almost like the mist of the fleeing eftan. She fell back, her hands going uselessly to her breast where there was no longer a jewel to save or strike. There was a small sound of explosion as if the air itself had burst open and then a fierce snarling.

She was looking at the wildcat, the animal which had led her into the whole of this venture. Its lips were curled back showing its sharp fangs, its fur stood erect, and its curved tail was a stiff brush.

"You . . . come—"

Two words in her mind, quavering as if the animal labored mightily to make her understand. It padded back and forth between her and the basin rim. She understood well enough; it wanted her to follow Wittle, to leap out—or in—aiming her body at the mountains below. She rubbed her eyes sure that this was an illusion, that surely the wildcat was not here, that it was part of her memory playing tricks on her.

"So—that is the way of it?" Yonan's voice startled her so that she started and nearly touched the rim. He was crawling like a sadly wounded beast toward the opening in the floor. She tried to reach him, to grasp his body and hold him back, for it was plain that he was about to do just what the cat wished.

Only, as she took a step toward him, the cat flew at her, one paw up, the talons extended to their farthest limit. Those hit her thighs and she stumbled back. It was too late. Yonan had reached the ridge of the basin, with both hands gripping there he pulled himself forward, leaving a small trail of blood on the stone. Over he dragged himself and was gone!

She looked to the gem, awaiting another flare of energy. But that did not come. Instead she felt again the rake of claws as the cat sprang at her for the second time. She gave way—stumbled back and to her terror felt herself go over.

There was no interval of dark, no feeling of falling that she could ever afterward remember. She opened her eyes and above her was the brilliant tapestry of the roof of feathers. Back in the Valley! Had it been a dream—her journey? Or was this the dream—a nightmare brought on by her fall?

Paws landed on her breast. There were large eyes turned upon her. The wildcat! And above her was Dahaun's face, her eyes also large and mirroring concern.

"This," Kelsie got one elbow bent, had lifted herself so far from the low mat bed on which she lay, "this is the Valley—"

She had not made a question of that but it would seem that Dahaun took it so, for she nodded.

"This is the Valley."

What was the truth then? Was there a second Estcarp and Escore in a basin within a forgotten temple, if temple that was, or merely the appearance of it strong enough to draw those attuned to its home?

"Perhaps," Dahaun was thought reading again, and Kelsie did not resent it.

"Wittle—the jewel—" she said.

As Yonan before her the Lady of Green Silences answered that. "She has what she sought—power unlimited, though not as she expected to choose it. But already the Dark is withdrawing—in that she does what she dreamed to do."

"And I? Or what is your dream—think upon that, sister." Dahaun arose and was gone. Only the purring cat kneading the front of her faded and soiled jerkin remained.

"For you," Kelsie said, "it is easy—you want only safe shelter for you and your family. For me—what do I want?"

By the light it was early evening, she had come out of the Valley and none had spoken to her. It seemed that she was to be left alone until she decided—decided what? She was not even sure of that.

She found herself going arrow straight to the stones— those blue, shining stones. There were no hounds, no Rider now. She had had enough confidence in Dahaun's words not to fear this night and she walked briskly until the stones stood before her.

Kelsie stepped forward until she could lay one hand on either side of that gate she could not see, which might never open again.

"Is it back?"

Startled she looked over her shoulder. Simon Tregarth stood there. For the first time she saw him out of armor, wearing the green dress of the Valley, his head bare of any helm.

"Can it be?" she asked.

He shrugged. "I never tried. I have heard it said, no. But of that I have had no proof. Do you want to try it?"

She looked back at the gate and thought of what might lie beyond it. There was none to have worried about her, grieved for her, and none she grieved for either.

"I am no witch—the jewel is broken," she said slowly.

"True enough. But that all power is bound to a gem, in that belief, too, there is error. You might be more than you expect—here."

"Here." She turned her back to the gate and looked about her. There was a yowl and the cat sprang from the bushes beyond and made a hunter's flying leap upon something small which ran in the grass.

"I think," Kelsie said, "that it is here." She took one step and then two and then began to run back to the Valley.

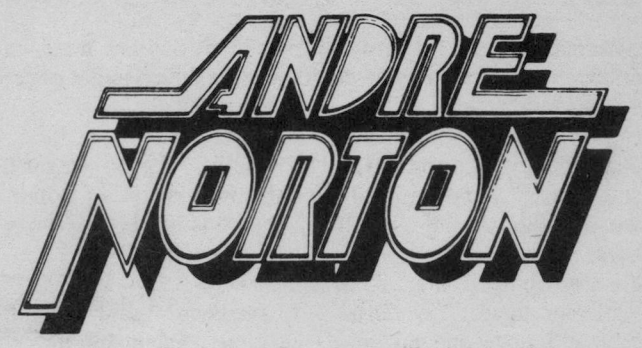

THE WITCH WORLD SERIES